EDMOND HAMILTON'S
CAPTAIN
FUTURE

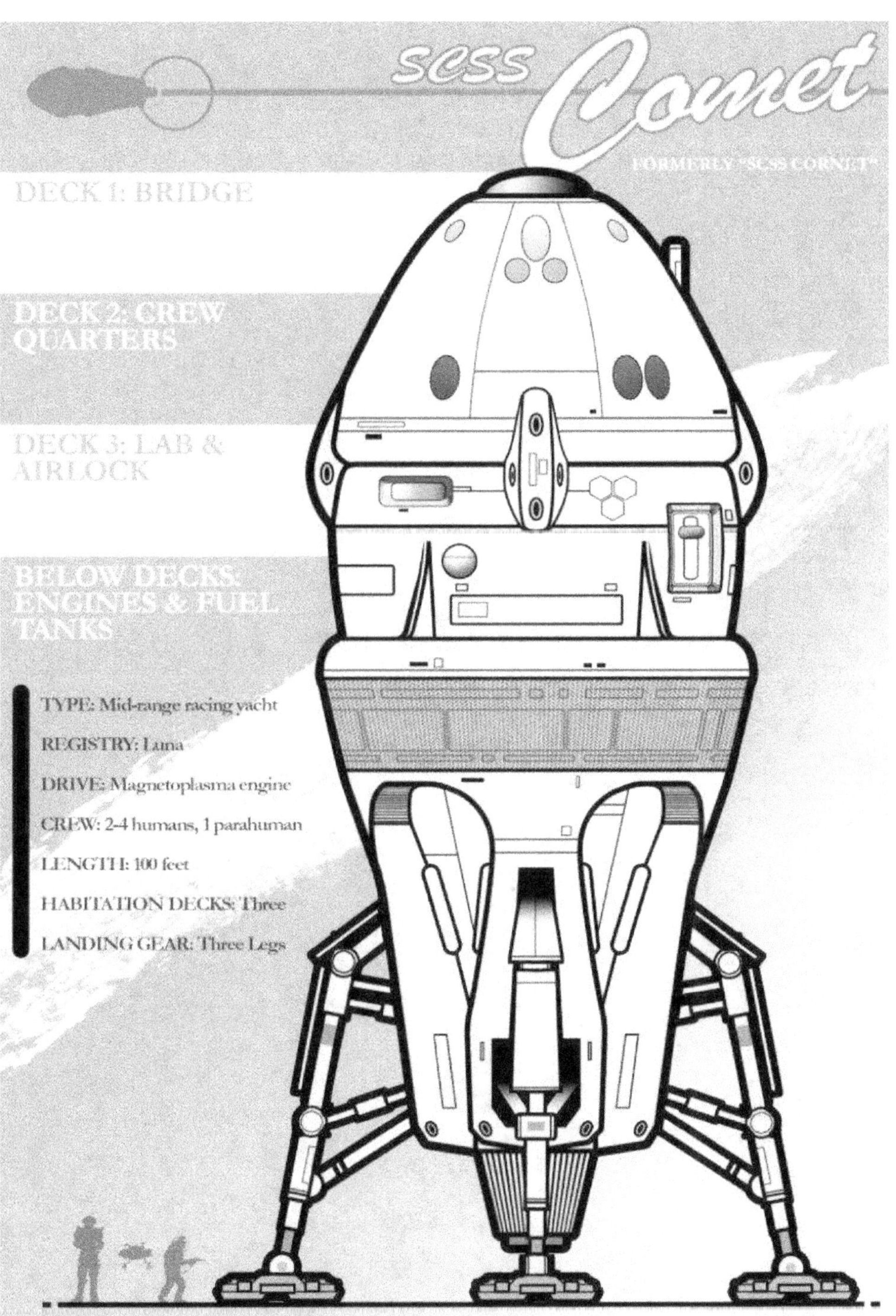

SCSS Comet
FORMERLY "SCSS CORNET"
DECK 1: BRIDGE
DECK 2: CREW QUARTERS
DECK 3: LAB & AIRLOCK
BELOW DECKS: ENGINES & FUEL TANKS
TYPE: Mid-range racing yacht
REGISTRY: Luna
DRIVE: Magnetoplasma engine
CREW: 2-4 humans, 1 parahuman
LENGTH: 100 feet
HABITATION DECKS: Three
LANDING GEAR: Three Legs
Illustration by Rob Caswell

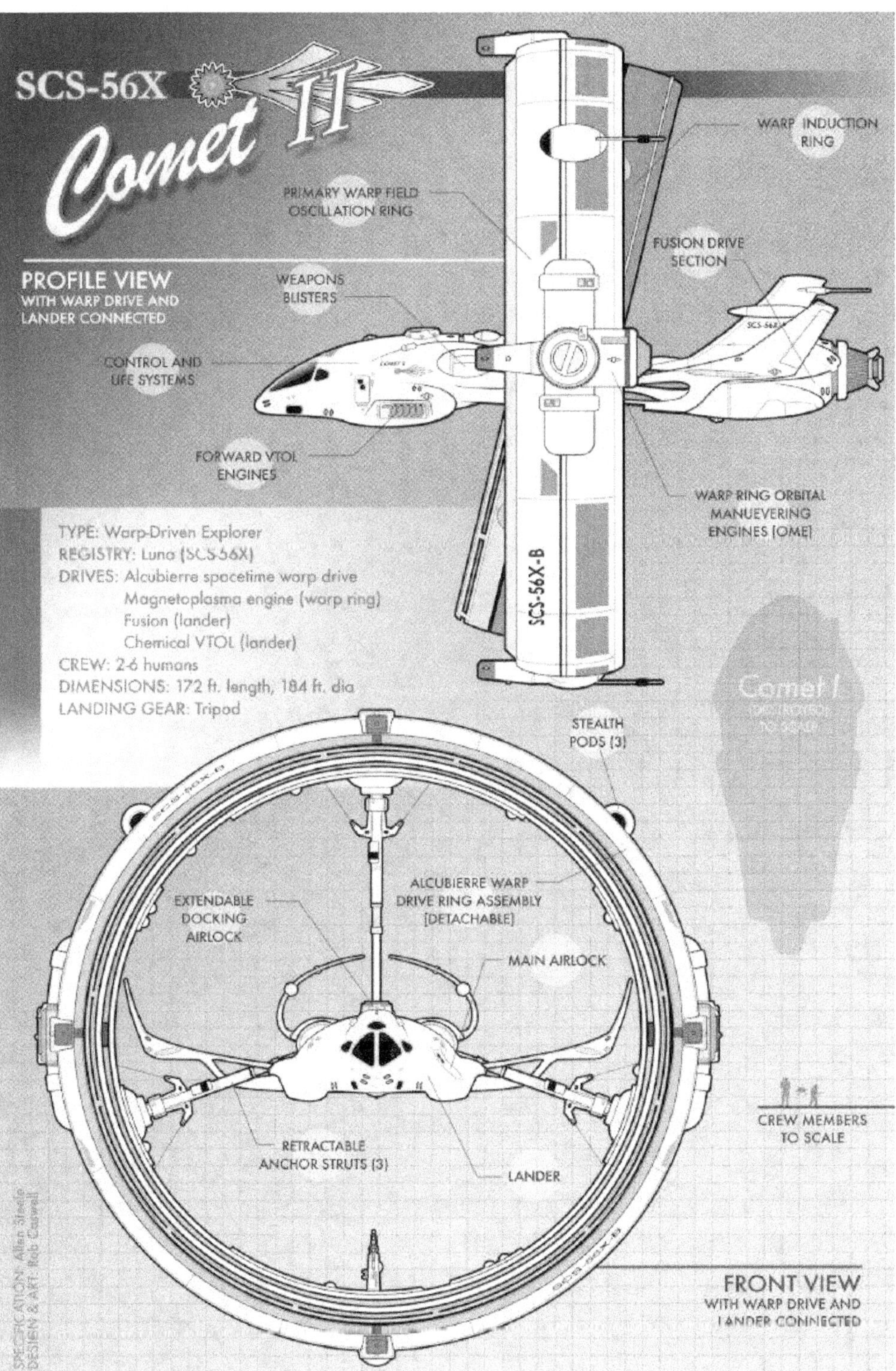

SCS-56X
Comet II

PROFILE VIEW
WITH WARP DRIVE AND
LANDER CONNECTED

PRIMARY WARP FIELD
OSCILLATION RING

WARP INDUCTION
RING

FUSION DRIVE
SECTION

WEAPONS
BLISTERS

CONTROL AND
LIFE SYSTEMS

FORWARD VTOL
ENGINES

WARP RING ORBITAL
MANUEVERING
ENGINES (OME)

SCS-56X-B

TYPE: Warp-Driven Explorer
REGISTRY: Luna (SCS-56X)
DRIVES: Alcubierre spacetime warp drive
        Magnetoplasma engine (warp ring)
        Fusion (lander)
        Chemical VTOL (lander)
CREW: 2-6 humans
DIMENSIONS: 172 ft. length, 184 ft. dia
LANDING GEAR: Tripod

Comet I

STEALTH
PODS (3)

ALCUBIERRE WARP
DRIVE RING ASSEMBLY
(DETACHABLE)

EXTENDABLE
DOCKING
AIRLOCK

MAIN AIRLOCK

CREW MEMBERS
TO SCALE

RETRACTABLE
ANCHOR STRUTS (3)

LANDER

FRONT VIEW
WITH WARP DRIVE AND
LANDER CONNECTED

SPECIFICATION: Allan Steele
DESIGN & ART: Rob Caswell

Captain Future in Love

(The Return of Ul Quorn, Book I)

by

Allen Steele

CONTENTS

Introduction:
Overture For A Space Opera

WELCOME TO BOOK ONE of *Edmond Hamilton's Captain Future*. If you're reading this on a screen, then you're participating in a publishing experiment, an attempt to produce a "hero pulp" of the kind that was once common in the 1930's and 40's, only this time in both paperback and ebook formats. Although this sort of "digital pulp" has been done before – Germany's long-running Perry Rhodan series made the jump to ebooks some years ago – this is (so far as we know) the first time it's been done by an American publisher.

It's also an attempt to revive and publish on a regular basis the new adventures of one of the great characters of the Pulp Era. Classic pulp heroes like Doc Savage, the Shadow, the Spider, and the Avenger have been successfully revived already...now it's Captain Future's turn. Elsewhere in this volume is a history of Edmond Hamilton's best-known creation; for now, though, know that we're picking up where Allen Steele's first Captain Future novel, *Avengers of the Moon*, left off, continuing the adventures of Curt Newton and the Futuremen.

This volume features "Captain Future in Love,", the first novella of a four-part story arc, *The Return of Ul Quorn*. Although each novella can be read on its own – beginning with Book Two, there will be a synopsis of the previous novellas for those who've come in late – together, they will comprise a novel-length narrative. Expect a couple of cliffhanger endings as we go along.

This series is traditional science fiction space opera, but it won't be old-fashioned. Although this version of Captain Future is fully authorized by the Edmond Hamilton estate, it's not the Captain Future of the 20th century. You won't find rocket tubes and blasters here; our female characters won't scream, run, and faint at the first sign of danger. Nor is this parody; Zapp Brannigan won't be joining us. What you will see is adult (but not X-rated) space adventure for those who want a break from "literary" science fiction. Nothing wrong with that kind of SF...it's just not what we're doing here. There's a place in the world for escapist entertainment; this is meant to be a spot where you'll find it.

If this initial four-part cycle is successful, *Edmond Hamilton's Captain Future* will continue. Three more novellas will follow the one you're about to begin, starting with Book Two, "The Guns of Pluto." So if you like what you're reading, please tell your friends and let them know where they can buy individual books or a membership in the planned Captain Future Society.

Have fun...and welcome to the future.

– the Author and Editors

Publisher's Introduction

DIVE RIGHT IN.

You don't really need an introduction to inform you that you are about to read something special. There's a good chance you already know this. I'm pretty confident of that assumption because we've given you four good reasons to assume specialness right on the cover.

There is a good reason why the names and words "Amazing Stories", "Amazing Selects", "Allen Steele," and "Captain Future," appear on that cover, not the least of which is the fact that this novella is a story about Captain Future written by none other than the award-winning author Allen Steele.

Those two facts alone ought to be enough to encourage you to plunk your quarter down for a chance to see the Egress. If you are still a bit hesitant, please allow this carnival barker a few more words.

One name I didn't mention was Edmond Hamilton. That name is on the cover too; if the name Allen Steele isn't enough for you to immediately ignore me and start turning pages, well, Edmond "Star Wrecker" Hamilton ought to be.

You see, Edmond was one of the earliest, if not the first, guy to realize that if you are playing around with faster than light travel, galaxy-spanning empires, and time-spanning millennia, your fleets are going to number in the tens of thousands of ships, your ships are going to be planet-sized, and your weapons are going to be capable of destroying entire star systems at one go.

Edmond, who died the same year that Star Wars was introduced to world-wide audiences, would have found the Death Star amusing. After all, he'd been writing about "galaxies far, far away" for fifty years by then. If asked about the movie, I'm pretty sure he'd have said something like, "Let me know when they come up with something original."

Which brings us back around to Captain Future. Edmond Hamilton created the Captain during the height of the pulp magazines, 1939 to be exact. Folks wanted heroes back then, and science fiction readers wanted science fiction heroes, and boy, did Edmond deliver. Some of the greatest names in the genre contributed epic stories to the *Captain Future Magazine*, Ray Bradbury, Henry Kuttner and Jack Williamson among them.

Still haven't turned the page? Well then, know this: Allen Steele has been known to write some great SF himself, and one of the things that inspired him to do so was Edmond Hamilton's Captain Future. Revamping and updating the Captain has been a dream and goal of Allen's for years.

Which means that what you are about to read is great science fiction; written by a great science fiction author, inspired by great science fiction; written by another great science fiction author!

Wait! I've not yet told you about the other two good reasons for reading this novella which appear on the cover: *"Amazing Stories"* and *"Amazing Selects."* The world's first science fiction magazine is going to be bringing you carefully selected, novella-length works under the *Amazing Stories Selects* banner. "Captain Future in Love" is just the first of what we hope will be a series of great reads: modern stories with a pulp feel.

– Steve Davidson
Publisher

Who is Captain Future?

Captain future is the *NOM DE GUERRE* of Curt Newton, adventurer, citizen-scientist, and troubleshooter for the Interplanetary Police Force (IPF) of the Solar Coalition. Although born on Earth, Curt was raised on the Moon, his very existence a closely-guarded secret following the murder of his parents, Roger and Elaine Newton, within their underground laboratory hidden beneath the floor of Tycho Crater.

Roger and Elaine, along with their teacher and mentor Simon Wright, were visionary scientists working on the development of a prototype android which they named Otho (an acronym for "Orthogenetic Transhuman Organism") that was intended to be a full-body replacement for the terminally ill Dr. Wright. It was their hope that, if Dr. Wright's mind could be successfully scanned into Otho's brain, he would be the first of many people who'd have their lives expanded indefinitely by such transfers.

However, shortly before Roger, Elaine, and Simon were about to enter the final phases of this project, they learned that their principal financial investor, Victor Corvo, had other plans for the new technology: selling it to the military to supply soldiers killed in combat with new bodies, in the process creating immortal armies. Seeing this as both unethical and dangerous, the three scientists decided to take the newborn Curt and flee to the Moon, where they'd finish Otho's development at remote Tycho Base, which Roger secretly built beneath the lunar surface with the aid of construction robots. In order to keep Corvo from learning where they'd gone, Roger Newton faked their death aboard his private racing yacht.

Upon arrival at Tycho Base, though, Simon Wright succumbed to the stress of the voyage from Earth. Fortunately, Roger and Elaine were able to preserve his brain and transfer it into a robotic, multi-functional drone. They also realized that one of the construction robots used to build the base had become a sentient and intelligent being who had taken the name of the company that manufactured him, Grag, as his own. Because it's useful to have an intelligent robot, Roger and Elaine decided to keep Grag while Simon learned to use the drone that his brain temporarily would occupy until Otho's body had finished its development within the experimental bioclast that Roger and Elaine had fashioned for the purpose.

Before this could happen, though, tragedy – and homicide – struck. Several months after the family's arrival on the Moon, Tycho Base had an unexpected visitor: Victor Corvo. Upon figuring out that Roger Newton faked the deaths of himself and his party, Corvo tracked them to Luna. And he didn't come alone, but instead brought with him a pair of killers-for-hire. During the confrontation that followed, Corvo had his assassins murder Roger and Elaine. However, Simon Wright witnessed the double-murder from his hiding place in Tycho's subsurface lair, where Roger had told him to take Curt when Corvo's ship landed. Simon ordered Grag to kill the assassins; however, Corvo managed to get away, leaving behind a bomb that devastated Tycho Base's above-ground facilities but didn't impact the hidden warrens below.

Having assumed that Roger Newton and his family were dead, Corvo fled back to Earth, unwittingly leaving behind Simon Wright, Curt Newton, Grag, and the soon-to-be-born Otho. Vowing to avenge the murders of Roger and Elaine, Simon took it upon himself to raise Curt in secrecy, training him for the day when he could track down Victor Corvo.

With Simon, Grag, and Otho as both his teachers and companions, Curt Newton spent the first decades of his life learning the skills he'd need for this task. In doing so Simon Wright – whom Otho and Curt nicknamed "the Brain" – gave Curt an appellation of his own: Captain Future, after the make-believe persona Curt fashioned for himself while playing in Tycho's underground passageways. The grown-up Curt was reluctant to use this childhood nickname, but the Brain insisted that he needed to keep his true identity a carefully-guarded secret as he pursued his campaign against Corvo, who, since his murder of Curt's parents, had become an elected member of the Solar Coalition Senate.

Eventually, Corvo was brought to justice. In doing so, Curt exposed a plot to destroy the Solar Coalition that Corvo had hatched along with his illegitimate son: Ul Quorn, the so-called Magician of Mars who was the leader of the Starry Messenger separatist movement. Curt refused to kill Senator Corvo, though, instead turning him over to the IPF. Once this was done, James Carthew – the President of the Solar Alliance whom Corvo had targeted for assassination – persuaded Curt to continue his newfound role as the Solar Coalition's troubleshooter.

Along with Lieutenant Joan Randall of the IPF (with whom Curt is not-so-secretly infatuated) and Simon, Otho, and Grag as his companions, Captain Future and the Futuremen – the name given by President Carthew to Curt's friends, teachers, and companions – became the protectors of law and justice on the high frontier.

THE RETURN OF UL QUORN

Prologue:

The Black Pirate and the King

I

IT WAS OFTEN SAID THAT one of the most romantic ways one could celebrate the New Year was by taking the Journey to the Rings cruise aboard the *Titan King*. Whether the experience was more spectacular than romantic is a matter of opinion, but there was no denying that, as interplanetary sojourns went, it was unique.

Framed against Saturn's immense northern hemisphere, the *Titan King* floated above its ring plane, hovering upside-down above the Enke Gap running through the A ring. Nearly seven hundred feet long, with a hemispherical observation dome at its bow and six fusion engines clustered at its stern, the liner was one of the largest vessels in space, capable of accommodating five hundred passengers and seventy-five crewmen. Its owners, the Kronos Line, proudly claimed that the *King's* luxury was matched only by the great ocean liners of old Earth, and they were probably right. Not even the line's other vessel, the *Hyperion Queen*, was quite as swank as her older and slightly larger brethren.

Within the observation dome, a ballet troupe danced weightless against the backdrop of Saturn's rings. As the ship's orchestra made its way through the fifth movement of Gustav Holst's *The Planets* – "Saturn, the Bringer of Old Age" – the troupe pirouetted above the stage in an intricately choreographed stardance, their skintight silver outfits catching the rings' harlequin colors as they caught each other by the hands and feet, twisted about, and flung their partner toward another dancer.

The dome's stage floor itself had become a vast mirror, reflecting the ring plane and casting the illusion that Saturn had a second set of rings below the first. Passengers occupied concentric rows of seats surrounding the floor, strapped in so that they wouldn't accidentally drift upward and disrupt the performance. At least, not until they were supposed to. At the close of the symphony's eerie seventh movement, "Neptune, the Mystic," the audience would be invited to unfasten their seat belts, discard their magnetic deck shoes, push off from the deck, and join the dancers floating about the dome. This would occur just a few minutes before 2400 GMT, when the year 2304 would come to a close and 2305 would begin.

Three-quarters of the way down the *Titan King* from the dome, the liner's command center rose as a wedge-shaped superstructure above the primary hull. Within the bridge, the fifth movement had just reached its ominous crescendo when the doors slid open and Captain Henri Lamont entered. The commanding officer had taken advantage of the lull following the station-keeping maneuver during the first movement ("Mars, the Bringer of War") to pay a brief visit to the galley and see if there was any dessert left over from the four-course dinner the passengers had enjoyed. Sated by a chocolate eclair and a squeezebulb of Napoleon brandy, Lamont returned to the bridge, ready to commence the liner's final maneuver of the evening, a diagonal flight through the Encke Gap to correspond with the last notes of *The Planets* and the first minutes of the New Year.

Captain Lamont strode across the command center to his chair, the magnetized soles of his shoes clicking softly against the deck. Although his younger officers preferred to get around by using the ornate brass handrails positioned throughout the liner, he tried to set an example to them by wearing his magshoes at all times, as dictated by Kronos Lines crew regulations. He'd just reached his seat when his aresian communications officer, Lieutenant Kars Kaastro, turned to him.

"Sir?" he said. "I believe we may have a small issue."

"A problem, Mr. Kaastro?" Settling into his chair, Lamont pulled the elastic straps around his waist. "Of what kind?"

"I've received a transmission from another vessel about twenty-two kilometers from our current position. A shuttle identifying itself as the *Skylark*, outbound from Mimas on its way to Iapetus. Priority ku-band signal, reporting failure of their life-support system."

Lamont frowned; this was the sort of unforeseen complication he detested. "Very well, put it on," he said, trying to hide his reluctance. He picked up his headset from where he'd left it on the armrest and fit it over his balding scalp. "*Skylark*, this is *Titan King*, Captain Henri Lamont speaking. I understand you're having trouble."

The voice that came through the headset was young, brisk, and aresian-accented. "Thank you for responding so promptly, Captain Lamont. This is Captain Os Mons of the *Skylark*. Apologies for bothering you at this time, but I'm afraid that my ship has developed a critical problem with its life support system. Specifically, the CO_2 scrubbers have broken down, causing the entire atmospheric system to go offline."

"Very sorry to hear this, Captain Mons," Lamont said. "If your ship's engines aren't similarly affected, I'm certain you'll be able to return to your point of origin without difficulty." While Iapetus was Saturn's outermost major satellite and therefore probably beyond range for a safe return, Mimas was a small shepherd moon orbiting just beyond the G ring.

An annoyed sigh. "A good suggestion, Captain, but my passengers and I are now on emergency airmasks. If you'll check with your navigator, you'll see that Mimas is nearly one-third of the way around Saturn from our current position. Again, I hate to impose upon you, but I'm afraid I have to request emergency rendezvous and docking."

"*Skylark*, stand by." Lamont muted his headset, then turned to his helmsman. "Mr. al-Sarakka, do you have a fix on the *Skylark*?"

"Yes, Captain." The big jovian put a wire-frame 3D projection of the two ships' respective positions on the holo screen above his station. "It's there," he said, pointing to a luminescent angular object hovering above the Encke Gap. "Not far. Can get here in –" his hairy eyebrows furrowed "– twenty-six point five minutes."

Lamont looked over at Eliza Watts, his executive officer. The young terran who was the *King's* second-in-command quietly shook her head. The rendezvous would blow their flight plan; it was impossible for the *Skylark* to dock with the *King* before the liner sailed through the gap at the symphony's climax. During the first movement, while the rising trumpets and strings masked the engine noise, the *King* had briefly swung about to fire its main engines and decelerate until it matched the orbital speed of the rings. Now that this had been accomplished, it was safe for the liner to penetrate the Encke Gap at a ninety-degree parabolic angle without risking collision with any of the ice chunks that made up the rings.

Yet there was no question that the *King* was obligated to rescue the *Skylark*. One of the principal laws of the Solar Coalition, dating back to the old United Nations space treaty of the twentieth century and, before that, centuries of maritime tradition, was that spacecraft always came to the aid of a stricken vessel and its crew. To do otherwise was unconscionable.

"Very well." Captain Lamont activated his headset again. "*Skylark*, this is *Titan King*. We'll maintain position and await your rendezvous. Our helmsman will transmit our coordinates and heading. Follow the beam and dock at the starboard landing bay. The hangar will be cleared for your arrival."

A short pause, then Captain Mons' voice returned. "Thank you, *King*. We're on course for rendezvous. ETA about twenty-five minutes, maybe a half-hour."

A quiet snort from al-Sarakka. Glancing at him, Lamont couldn't help but notice the smirk all but hidden within the helmsman's thick black beard. Jovians were notoriously dismissive of anyone who wasn't as precise about mathematical figures as they were, and even more contemptuous of any spacer who had to ask for help. Lamont didn't say anything, though, and without being told, Mr. al-Sarakka began adjusting the liner's flight plan.

"We copy, *Skylark*," Lamont said. "We'll be waiting for you. *Titan King* over and out."

The captain swiveled his chair so that he could see another overhead screen. In the orchestra pit beneath the observation dome stage, the conductor was leading the orchestra through the opening bars of the sixth movement, "Uranus, the Magician." He wouldn't be pleased when he discovered that this New Year's Eve performance of *The Planets* would be lacking the finale's visual element, but Lamont knew better than to interrupt him while he was working. He'd tell the maestro later, and brace himself for the ire of an artist denied.

"Mr. Kaastro, please apprise Titan Station of the change in flight plan and inform them that we'll be returning to schedule once the *Skylark* has been retrieved." Lamont turned to al-Sarakka again. "Harl, as soon as the shuttle is aboard and the deck crew informs us that it's been secured, commence the dive maneuver. We'll be a few minutes late for the end of the performance, but we can still give 2305 a proper kick-off."

The helmsman's only response was an annoyed grunt. Lamont glanced at Eliza. She didn't say anything, but she smiled and gave him an approving nod. Lamont nodded in return, then clasped his hands together behind his head and lay back in his seat to enjoy the rest of the symphony.

No crisis. Just a small glitch in an otherwise perfect cruise.

II

THE *SKYLARK* WAS ONE OF THOSE UGLY, bug-like space vehicles that were used as workhorses among Saturn's moons. This one obviously served as a ferry, for just forward of the aft nuclear engines was a detachable passenger module. Apparently, the *Skylark* had been transporting people from Mimas to Titan Station when the life support system broke down. Although Captain Mons hadn't reported any injuries, Captain Lamont took the precaution of sending the ship's doctor down to the shuttle bay.

Lamont asked his XO if she'd go down there as well, so Eliza was in the hangar's observation cupola when the *Skylark* made its emergency landing. The *King*'s physician, Sean Dacus, was standing beside her; he'd brought his medical bag and a trauma 'bot from the infirmary just in case they were needed. They watched as the *Skylark*'s spidery landing gear touched down, and as soon as the hangar crew chocked the wheels and the deck was repressurized, Eliza and Sean came down from the cupola.

As the hatch on the passenger pod's port side opened, Eliza felt a slight motion at her feet. Like Sean, she was wearing magshoes; only the hangar crew were allowed to float about in zero-g. It was as if the hangar was an elevator that had suddenly begun to descend. She knew what this was: the *Titan King* had commenced its dive through the Encke Gap.

Eliza glanced at her watch: sure enough, it was 00:04 GMT, four minutes into January 1, 2305. In the observation dome, the orchestra would have concluded its annual performance of *The Planets* just a few minutes ago. The braver passengers would be floating about the dome among the dancers, while stewards served champagne bulbs to those who'd remained in their seats. Almost everyone in the bow were unaware that, while they were enjoying the New Year's festivities, the *King* had come to the aid of a stricken spacecraft.

Indeed, even Titan Station wouldn't learn of the rescue until after the liner crossed the Encke Gap. Saturn's rings aren't very thick – only thirty feet on average – but spacecraft passing through them experienced a brief communications blackout when their forward deflector arrays were activated. The deflectors ionized the gap's thin layer of dust and ice particles and brushed them safely aside, but they also played havoc with telemetry. So until the *Titan King* was well south of the ring plane, the liner would be incommunicado with the spacehab in orbit above Titan, if only for a few minutes.

None of this was on the XO's mind, though, as a couple of deckhands clipped a ladder into place below the shuttle hatch. A brief pause, then a passenger emerged: an aresian woman, black haired and tall, her red skin only a shade lighter than the elegantly brocaded cape she wore about her shoulders. She wore magshoes over her knee boots, and as she stepped down the ladder, she removed the airmask that covered the lower part of her face. Eliza now saw that she was stunningly beautiful, possessing a sort of mystic radiance that reminded her of a sunset on the Martian drylands.

Behind her came an assortment of passengers. Baseline *Homo sapiens* from Earth mainly, but also a few *Homo cosmos*: two more aresians, both men; an aphrodite, ebony-skinned, hairless, and thin; a massive, hirsute jovian who looked as if he could bend Harl al-Sarakka like a pretzel. They were genetically-altered cousins of the human race, their ancestors genengineered to inhabit other worlds of the solar system, fundamentally human yet alien at the same time. All wore magshoes as well as emergency airmasks that they removed as soon as they disembarked from the shuttle. Oddly, they also carried shoulder bags, as if they were reluctant to leave their belongings aboard the *Skylark*. Eliza hoped they weren't expecting passenger accommodations. The staterooms were all occupied, and there were no third-class bunks aboard the *Titan King*.

"No one seems worse for wear," Dr. Dacus murmured as he watched the last few emerge. "Looks like everyone put on their masks in time."

Eliza gave a distracted nod. She'd just noticed something else: although the passengers had left the shuttle, the pilots didn't seem to be among them, for none of the dozen men and women gathered on the deck wore standard-issue skinsuits of a spacecraft's flight crew. Glancing at the *Skylark's* spherical bow module, she caught a glimpse of figures moving within the cockpit. All right, so the pilot and co-pilot were still aboard…but why were they taking so long to leave?

The woman who'd come down the ladder first had paused to look about as if taking in the hangar deck. Then her eyes turned toward Eliza, and as if recognizing an old acquaintance she smiled warmly and, extending her hands, strolled across the deck to the XO.

"Eliza!" she exclaimed, taking Eliza's hands in her own. Even for an aresian, she was unusually tall; Eliza had to look up at her. "How lovely to see you! Happy New Year!"

"Uhh…yes, Happy New Year." Eliza accepted the greetings with uncertain politeness. As hard as she tried, she couldn't remember having ever met this woman. "I'm so sorry, but…do we know each other? I don't –"

"Of course not, silly!" The aresian woman beamed at her as this was the most obvious thing. "But I know who **you** are, and that's all the matters. Here, let me show you… –."

As she spoke, the woman dropped Eliza's hands. Her right hand disappeared for an instant within the scarlet folds of her cloak, reappearing a moment later holding a particle beam pistol.

"Ta-da!" she announced. "Look what I have!"

Astonished, the XO stared at the gun pointed at her chest, then looked at the others who'd just disembarked from the *Skylark*. Each had reached into their shoulder bags and produced particle beam pistols or rifles. The two aresians were covering the deckhands while the jovian had his PBP trained on Sean. The remaining shuttle passengers had already discarded their bags and were sprinting past them, heading for the deck hatch leading to the rest of the ship.

"I don't suppose you'd like to tell me who you are or what you think you're doing?" Struggling to remain calm, Eliza started to raise her hands.

"Oh, stop it...you don't need to do that." Taking a step back, the aresian woman motioned with her gun toward Eliza's hands. The XO obligingly dropped them; apparently these people were already aware that the liner's crew customarily went about their duties unarmed. "You'll have to forgive me if I don't tell you my name," she went on, "but the rest should be obvious. I'm taking your ship." She paused. "Strike that. **We're** taking your ship. I forgot my lover."

As if on cue, another person emerged from the shuttle. Hearing his footsteps on the ladder, Eliza turned to look at him ...and gasped, not quite believing what she was seeing.

The tall figure who came down the ladder was dressed entirely in black, a kind of black that seems to absorb the light surrounding it. From the skintight cowl that covered his entire head to the toes of his magshoes, he wore a one-piece bodysuit that was as dark as space itself. Judging from his height and powerful, broad-chested build, he appeared to be an aresian, but his mask made positive identification impossible. The only color in his outfit was the scarlet lining of the long cape that billowed around his shoulders, and the narrow red lenses of the pair of eyes that blazed from his mask.

Followed by an albino selenite who Eliza assumed to be the shuttle pilot, he walked over to her. When he spoke, she recognized the voice as the same one she'd heard earlier over the comlink, claiming an emergency and requesting assistance.

"Good morning," he said, his tone firm yet not unpleasant, with a mild aresian accent. "I presume you're Eliza Watts, the executive officer of this fine vessel." He gave her a second to answer; when she didn't, he went on anyway. "I'll also assume that Captain Lamont is aware of our presence and has reached the logical conclusion that we're hijacking his ship."

Eliza didn't reply, but had to suppress the shudder that went through her. Whoever these people were, they'd studied their target in advance, and had learned enough about the *Titan King* and its crew to know not only the names of its senior officers but also the fact that there were vidcams in the shuttle bay. Someone on the bridge would have been watching what was going on down here, even if Captain Lamont himself was concentrating on the Encke Gap fly-through.

She tried not to smile. Although a hijacking had always been considered unlikely, certain security procedures had been put in place on the off chance that it ever occurred.

As if to confirm this, a loudspeaker on the forward hangar wall suddenly erupted in a loud **arrou-gaah! arrou-gaah!** The Black Pirate – it was the name Eliza gave him, and none suited him better – raised his hands to his ears while his female cohort looked around as if trying to locate the source of the noise. A second later, Lamont's voice blared over the speaker:

"All passengers and non-essential crew members, report immediately to your designated lifeboats! Repeat…all passengers and non-essential crew, proceed at once to your designated lifeboats immediately!"

"Damn!" The pirate had his hands clamped over his ears. "Does it really have to be that loud?" He looked over at his companion. "Can't you shoot that thing or something? It's giving me a headache."

The aresian woman nodded and took aim at the speaker. A single shot silenced both the alarm and the captain's voice, and the Black Pirate lowered his hands. "That's better. All right, now, where were we? Oh, yes…" He pointed to Dr. Dacus and the two deckhands. "You, you, and you…do as your captain says. Find your lifeboats and get aboard."

Sean stared at the pirate. "You don't want us to –?"

"Stay? Not unless you want to join up…do you? No? Then get out of here. Scram." The masked intruder dismissed the doctor with a flip of a gloved hand. Sean hesitated, then strode quickly toward the hatch, followed closely by the deckhands. The pirate watched them go, then turned to Eliza again. "Very well, my good lady, if you'll escort me to the bridge, I'd greatly appreciate it."

Eliza forced a smile, even as she tried to get past her own astonishment that this act of piracy apparently didn't include taking hostages. "Certainly, Os Mons…that **is** your name, isn't it?"

"Actually, it's his." The pirate cocked his head toward the shuttle pilot. "I just borrowed it while I was talking to your captain."

"So I take it you don't want anyone knowing who you are." Eliza looked at his female companion. "At least you've got the courage to show your face. Only a coward would wear a mask."

The smirk on the aresian woman's face disappeared, replaced by a menacing glare. She started to speak, but the Black Pirate silenced her with a lifted finger. "It's only a small insult, my dear, and one we can live with." The scarlet eyes within the mask revealed no emotion, yet Eliza could hear a tinge of laughter in his voice. "Besides," he added, "everyone will know our names…soon."

III

Henri Lamont had just enough time to sound the alarm and order all passengers and non-essential crew to the lifeboats before the command center's security doors, which had automatically shut at the touch of an appropriate button, slammed open with the bang of an explosive charge. The pirates had come prepared for everything, it seemed.

Three armed men rushed into the compartment. The only security officer who'd managed to make it to the bridge went down before he could get off a shot; the hole that had been burned through his heart was still smoking several minutes after he'd hit the floor, by which time Eliza Watts had returned, accompanied by the pirate chief and his female accomplice.

Lamont was standing beside his chair when the Black Pirate came in. The captain had risen to his feet when the assault team had reached the command center and breached the security door, and had been allowed to remain standing even though the rest of the bridge crew had been ordered to remain at their posts. The only exception was Kars Kaastro, who'd been yanked away from the com station at gunpoint and firmly told not to touch his board at risk of his life. The captain glared at the masked figure who strolled over to him and offered a handshake.

"Captain Lamont…what a pleasure to meet you. Happy New Year." The Black Pirate sighed when Lamont refused to take his hand. "Oh, come now. Is a little courtesy such a hard thing to accept?"

"You've come aboard my ship under false pretenses, terrorized my passengers, taken control of my bridge, killed one of my men –"

"Two." The pirate shook his head apologetically. "Another member of your security team attempted to stop us in the A Deck corridor on our way here. M'lady was forced to liquidate him." He glanced at his companion. "Tell the captain you're sorry."

"I'm sorry," said the aresian woman.

"At any rate…" The buccaneer looked past Lamont at the forward windows. Saturn's rings were now apparently below the liner's keel, the Encke Gap closer and wider than before. "Oh, excellent! You completed the maneuver even while your ship was being taken by my forces." He looked over at Harl al-Sarakka, who was still seated at the helm. "My compliments, Mr. al-Sarakka. Beautiful flying. I always admire grace under pressure. I only regret that I was too busy to witness it myself." He turned to one of the men who'd taken control of the bridge.

"And you managed to prevent the com officer from transmitting a distress signal? Please tell me that you did."

"Yes, sir." The terran who'd told Kaastro that he'd be shot if he so much as laid a finger on his instruments nodded an affirmative. "They were still passing through the gap when we came in, so nothing got out. Of that, I'm certain."

"Excellent. Well done. And the lifeboats?"

"Still in their launch tubes." The hijacker pointed to a monitor screen above the life-support station. It displayed a view of the promenade deck between the observation dome and the primary hull. Dozens of passengers, angry and confused, were crowded into the narrow corridor, impatiently jostling one another as stewards sought to load them aboard the *King's* lifeboats through circular hatches lining both sides of the corridors. "Shall I send our people down to stop them?"

His leader studied the screen for a moment. "No. That's five hundred or so fewer people we have to worry about, more if we include non-essential crew…stewards, cooks, housekeeping staff and so on." He glanced at the life-support officer; his panel included the master control for the lifeboat tubes. "Don't jettison them yet," he instructed. "I want to make sure everyone we don't need finds a boat and gets aboard."

The Black Pirate returned his gaze to Captain Lamont, then let it sweep across the half-dozen bridge officers gathered around them. "I might even include some of the people here," he added, "if you're willing to cooperate."

Lamont swallowed. The crew lifeboats were only two decks down from the bridge. Unlike the ones the passengers were fighting over, those bays were uncrowded, the crew well-drilled in evacuation procedures. He could have the bridge crew out of harm's way in a minute. The captain found himself gazing at Eliza; she was trying not to show it, but it was clear that she was frightened. Lamont was very fond of his young XO, and the last thing he wanted was for her to get hurt.

"What is it that you want?" Lamont asked, looking the Black Pirate straight in the eye as best he could. "You've got my ship. Isn't that enough?"

"Well…not quite." Turning away from him, the masked hijacker gazed about the command center. "If I may have your attention please," he addressed the rest of the bridge crew, "I'd like to propose to each of you an opportunity. In the old days of the Caribbean, when buccaneers like Black Bart and Calico Jack attacked the sailing ships of the English, French, and Spanish, they would customarily offer their captives a choice…join up or be cast away. I'm tendering the same offer to you today."

"You must be joking!" Lamont snapped.

He didn't intend to blurt that out, but what the Black Pirate said was so absurd that he couldn't help himself. The pirate chief didn't respond, but instead looked over his shoulder to give the captain a long, hard stare that made him realize that silence was probably the best policy. Assured of no more interruptions, the man in black returned his attention to the bridge crew.

"This is no joke," he went on, "and here is why. Although I have experienced spacers among my men, none of them have operated a vessel this size. Most of your major control systems are automated, but nonetheless I could use your assistance for the task I have in mind…and yes, there is a specific reason why I've chosen to take the *King*. So I'll need the help of men and women who know how to fly this ship."

As he spoke, the pirate strolled about the command center, pausing at each station to speak one-to-one with each of the crew members. "We are pirates, this is true," he continued, "but we're not bloodthirsty, nor are we terrorists. Like our predecessors who carried letters of marque giving them license to carry out their actions, we have a sponsor, too. I assume you've heard of Starry Messenger, and that you know what they stand for."

When he said this, the bridge crew cast meaningful glances at one another. Lamont felt a chill. Yes, everyone knew about Starry Messenger, the interplanetary separatist group – a self-described "liberation movement" – dedicated to wresting control of Mars, the major asteroids and Galilean moons, and other inhabited worlds of the outer solar system from the Solar Coalition. Three years ago, a Starry Messenger plot to bring about an armed insurrection on Mars had been quelled by the Interplanetary Police Force and the Solar Guard…and in particular, the mysterious adventurer known as Captain Future, who'd also exposed the involvement of the former senator of the Lunar Republic, Victor Corvo.

Since then, Starry Messenger had gone underground, its surviving members emerging only occasionally to stage another "political action" against SolCol. Each effort had been defeated by Captain Future and his Futuremen, who apparently operated out of a secret base somewhere on the Moon. But as many times as Starry Messenger had lost, or however many of their members had either been killed or shipped off to Pluto, the organization had never given up…and Lamont was aware that there were quite a few who quietly sided with their reasons, if not their methods.

"So consider this an invitation to join a great cause," the pirate chief said. "I cannot tell you now where we'll be going or what we'll be doing, but I assure you that your efforts will be rewarded. I won't lie to you…the journey ahead is dangerous, and without doubt we'll be opposed. But if we're successful – and I believe we will be – then you'll be remembered by history not as a turncoat or a traitor but as a freedom fighter. A liberator of worlds."

By then, his tour of the command center had brought him back to where he'd started, standing beside Lamont. "Captain, I'm afraid this offer doesn't extend to you. Many apologies, but my plans dictate that I must take you as our hostage. However, I assure you that you'll be treated well, so long as you obey my instructions and behave yourself." He looked at the rest of the bridge crew. "Anyone who chooses not to join us will be allowed to board the lifeboats. Once aboard, you'll be safely released. I have no desire to keep prisoner anyone who might give me trouble later, nor am I a bloodthirsty man."

Stepping away from Lamont, the Black Pirate clasped his hands behind his back. "I'll give you a minute to think it over. Anyone who wishes to join us, come stand beside me. Otherwise, you need to do nothing more than remain where you are until my men escort you down to the lifeboats."

He lowered his eyes and regarded the floor for a full minute. Then he raised his head again.

"Now choose," he said.

THE RETURN OF UL QUORN

Book One:

Captain Future In Love

I

AFTER BECOMING AN ADULT, in just a few years Curt Newton was famous throughout the solar system as Captain Future, the red-haired adventurer and champion of justice. Long before then, though, he was a lonely boy with a tragic past. For everyone except his companions, the Futuremen, his childhood was as mysterious as the man himself. So far as the citizens of the Solar Coalition were concerned, Captain Future was a hero, nothing more, nothing less.

But even lonely boys can fall in love.

II

NOW (MARCH 12, 2305)...

"Engine arm," Curt said.

A faint beep from the overhead instrument panel. "Affirmative, engine armed," Simon responded from behind Curt's seat.

"Communications check."

Otho's voice through the cockpit speaker: "Com check, one, two, three. Do you copy?"

"We copy, *Comet*." Curt reached up to snap a couple of switches. "Switching to internal power. Detach umbilical."

A slight jar as the external power cable separated from the recon pod's spherical hull. He checked the voltage readouts to make sure there was no drop-off that would indicate poorly charged batteries. Satisfied, he lowered his arms to his sides and curled his gloved hands around the control bars. "Open hatch and lower trapeze."

"Hatch open," Otho replied from the *Comet's* flight deck. A moment later, a circular hatch in the *Comet's* underbelly bisected. "Trapeze down." Sunlight streamed into the pod bay as the small, one-man craft was lowered by its docking trapeze. The pod descended until it was clear of its mothership, then clamps along the top of the trapeze snapped open from the docking rungs on the pod's upper fuselage.

"Trapeze disengaged," Otho said. "Pod ready for deployment."

"Confirmed," Simon said. "We're go for launch."

"Thanks, *Comet*," Curt replied. "Recon pod launching." He pushed both bars forward and squeezed the recessed triggers in their hand grips, and the port and starboard engine nacelles tilted forward and silently fired. With barely a shudder, the pod slowly fell away from the *Comet II*. Now that the view through the pod's bombardier window was no longer obstructed by the hatch, Curt could clearly see where they were.

Venus lay below, a burnt-orange globe swirled by the dark tan whorls of its upper cloud layer. The *Comet II* was in low orbit above the planet, altitude 320 kilometers, but now that the pod was away the ship would soon ascend to a higher parking orbit about 1,200 km above Venus. Deftly twisting the control bars, Curt fired the maneuvering thrusters to rotate the pod until he was looking up at the ship. The *Comet II* had aerobraked in the Venusian upper atmosphere upon arrival, and Curt wanted to make sure his ship was unscratched.

The *Comet II* bore little resemblance to the original *Comet*, an old racing yacht he'd sacrificed on Mars three years ago. Built to Curt Newton and Simon Wright's specifications at the Solar Guard shipyard on the Moon, the replacement was larger and more sophisticated. The main part of the ship was a winged landing craft 172 feet long, equipped with both fusion engines and, for atmospheric travel, scramjets. This part of the ship, by itself, was unique; no other spacecraft in the solar system looked even remotely like the *Comet*'s second iteration. Everyone in the system who caught even a glimpse of the *Comet II* recognized it as Captain Future's ship.

But that was only half of the craft. The tips of the *Comet*'s sleek wings folded up, thereby allowing the lander to fit within a broad, double-sided torus. Now temporarily connected to the lander's midsection, the 184-foot wide torus contained the *Comet*'s Alcubierre warp drive, capable of boosting the ship to near-light-speed. Only Solar Guard ships possessed this highly-classified technology. When the *Comet* reached its destination, the lander would detach from the warp module and descend to the surface, leaving the torus – rendered invisible within it own light-deflecting fantome field – in orbit until the ship and its crew returned from their mission.

An appropriately futuristic craft for Captain Future and the Futuremen. Curt had to admit to himself that he wasn't really all that concerned about the hull. Fact was, he just liked looking at his ship.

A metal claw reached forward from behind his seat to gently prod his shoulder. "If you're done admiring your toy," Simon said drily, "perhaps we can get on with our mission."

Curt glanced over his shoulder to see Simon's eyestalks peering at him. "I thought you were my favorite toy…ow!" Curt winced as the manipulator claw slapped the back of his neck above his suit's helmet ring. "Okay, sorry! Just kidding!"

"You'd better be." Simon withdrew his manipulator; his eyestalks, though, continued to hover above Curt's shoulders. "Remember that your seat is equipped with an emergency ejection system. And while I'm interfaced with the pod, I can override the manual controls any time I want."

Curt knew that Simon was joking, but there was no sense in pushing his luck. Although the pod was technically a one-seater, it had been designed so that it could also accommodate one passenger in particular: the Brain, as Curt and Otho had nicknamed Dr. Simon Wright many years ago. Simon was back there now, the saucer-shaped drone containing his living brain securely strapped against the rear bulkhead. A slender cable connected his neural-net interface to the pod's flight systems, allowing Simon to effectively act as co-pilot. Curt usually flew the pod by himself, but for this particular mission he needed help.

"All right, enough fun." Curt fired the maneuvering thrusters and turned the little craft away from the *Comet*. "Time for Captain Future and the Futuremen to come to the rescue."

"Again," Otho added.

"Again," he agreed. His smile quickly faded. "All right, then…beginning communications blackout. Will resume contact when we arrive. All set, Otho?"

"Affirmative. At T-plus ten, we'll park the drive and commence final approach and docking with Venera Stratos. See you at the rendezvous point, chief."

"Roger that. Captain Future, over and out." Curt switched off the comlink. "All right, Brain…take us in."

III

OF THE ORBITAL COLONIES scattered across the solar system, Venera Stratos was one of the largest. It had to be; it was practically a world in itself.

Long before humankind became a spacefaring civilization, it was clear that, despite its proximity to Earth, Venus would never become the lure that Mars always was. Men looked at Mars and saw a planet that could be settled and, in time, transformed into a habitable world. But Venus was untameable. With an average surface temperature of $860°F$ and a toxic carbon-dioxide atmosphere whose surface pressure was ninety times greater than Earth's, it daunted even the most ambitious schemes for terraforming. People often compared Venus to Hell, but the comparison wasn't entirely accurate. The circles of Dante's *Inferno* would have been a relief to someone recently arrived from Venus.

And yet, down there within its cloud-shrouded volcanic plains were enough precious metals and carbon compounds to supply the needs of the entire system, including the Solar Coalition's generations-long effort to turn Mars into a new home for the human race. Venus was a planet-size mother lode of materials humankind needed to sustain the interplanetary civilization it had become. The trick was getting to it.

The Venusian surface was uninhabitable, yes, but the first probes to parachute through the clouds and make soft landings managed to survive, if only for a few minutes. This demonstrated that it was possible for machines to be made that would be capable of withstanding the heat and pressure. Above the twelve-mile-thick layers of clouds, high in the stratosphere where the air was clear and the sky was blue, lay a temperate zone where the average daytime temperature was only about $165°F$...still hot, but at least not hot enough to melt lead. And because Venus's gravity was a little less than Earth's, the costs of lifting a payload into orbit were not prohibitive, particularly if it was from the equatorial region.

Venera Stratos was the solution.

Located in a circular equatorial orbit 1,100 kilometers above Venus, the colony consisted primarily of two large but unequal spheres joined by a small one at the center. The largest sphere, called Venera, was an O'Neill Type 1 spacehab, a Bernal sphere 500 meters in diameter, whose circular windows and slated outside mirrors channeled sunlight into a bubble-like outside-in world inhabited by several thousand aphrodite colonists.

The second largest sphere was Stratos, an industrial space facility, one of the largest in the system. It superficially resembled Venera, but its lack of windows

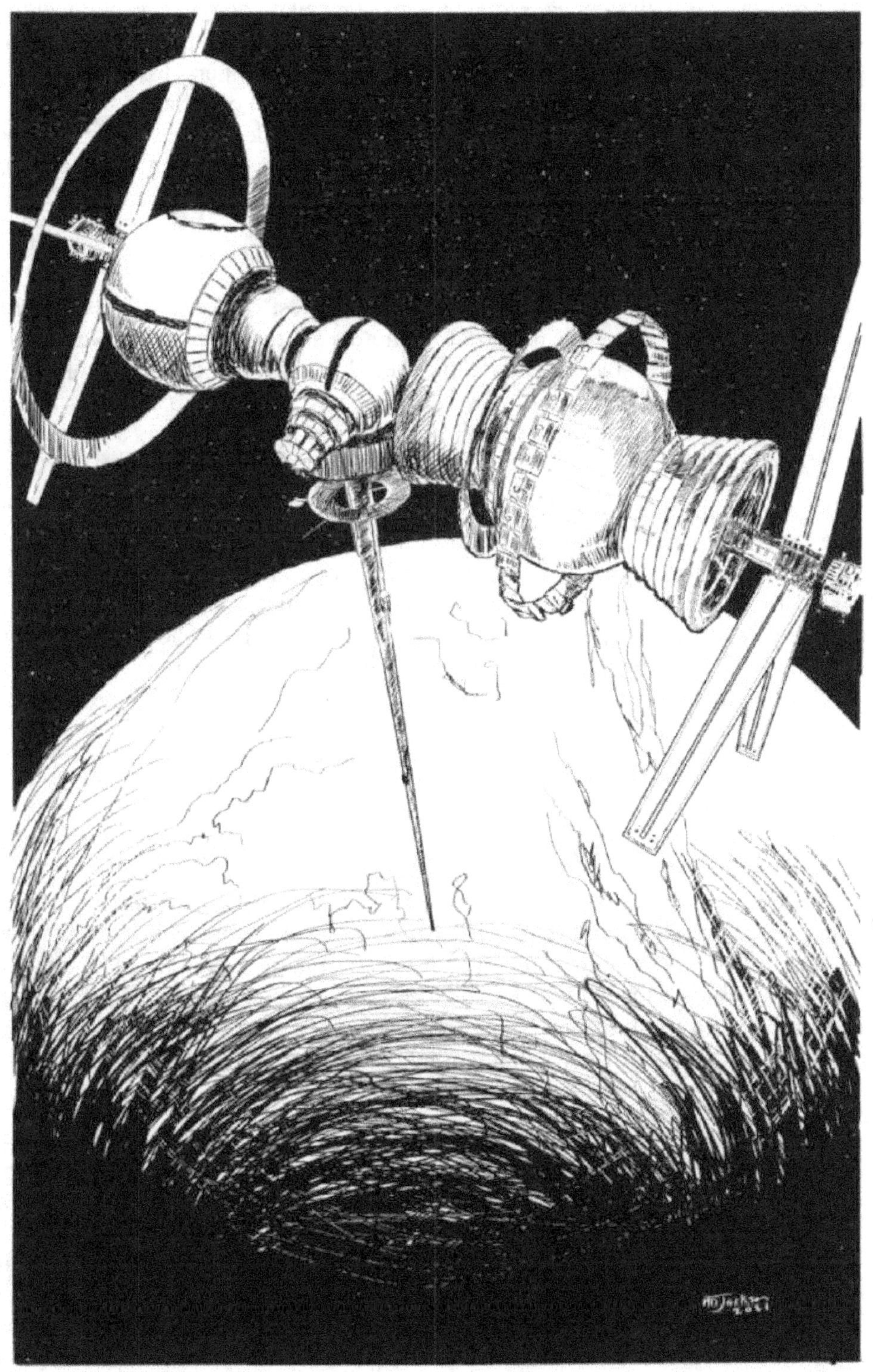

and mirrors, along with the heat radiators and wing-like solar arrays, showed that it wasn't another hollow world, but instead a 250-meter sphere whose onion-layer decks were parked with the necessary heavy machinery for refining raw materials brought up from the Venusian surface. Most of Stratos' inhabitants worked here, a company-town relationship made palatable by the aphrodist social system. Enterprise Amtor owned Venera Stratos, sure, but since the Venusian Socialist Republic owned Enterprise Amtor, that made every native aphrodite both a citizen and a shareholder.

Somehow, the aphroditic version of Marxist socialism worked just as reliably as the colony's third component. The smallest of Venera Stratos' three major modules was a spherical hub, 130 meters in diameter. However, while Venera and Stratos rotated clockwise on their long axes to give the colony an internal 1-g gravity at their respective equators, the hub rotated counter-clockwise on immense gimbals at a slower, more stately rate, thus allowing the rotating space elevator at its center to fulfill its purpose.

Woven from ultrastrong strands of graphene derived from atmospheric carbon, the elevator – technically called a rotavator, although people usually referred to it as the skyhook, or sometimes Scoopy Skyhook – was a rotating tether with uneven ends. The longer of the two ends, 1,080 kilometers long, entered the Venusian upper atmosphere three times during each orbit Venera Stratos made around the planet. This end would slowly descend to an altitude of twenty kilometers, putting it above the dense clouds and the hellish surface heat trapped beneath them.

Because of Venus' extremely slow axial rotation and corrosive atmosphere, a space elevator directly from the surface to orbit was all but impossible. Instead, mining operations were conducted by enormous mining machines teleoperated by aphrodites on the colony. The raw materials extracted from the native regolith were loaded aboard cargo carriers, which in turn were lifted off the surface by remote-piloted freight dirigibles, their carbon-frame skeletons and hydrogen gas cells capable of withstanding the planet's extreme pressure. Once above the clouds, the airships cruised to the established rendezvous points along the equator. There, they would use thrusters to hold stationary and wait for the next arrival of the skyhook and the claw-manipulators that would attach the cargo carriers to the elevator and lift them into the dark sky above.

As the tether ascended, the cargo carriers traveled up the rotavator to the hub, where their contents were unloaded and hauled into Stratos. Here, raw material was separated, refined, processed, and transformed into all variety of finished items, ranging from spaceship hullplates to nanoelectronics. The finished products were then loaded back aboard the cargo containers and carried back to the hub, where they traveled down the other end of the tether. The skyhook's short end, only 550 kilometers long, never reached the atmosphere. Instead, once the containers reached the spaceport at its end, they were loaded aboard the planetary freighters docked there, which in turn would be given a gravity-assist slingshot launch once the rotarvator completed its revolution. From there, the freighters would be flung outward to Earth, Luna, Mars, and points beyond.

Venera Stratos took many years to conceive and build, yet even as the Solar Coalition and Enterprise Amtor were working out the engineering details, plans were also made for the colony's eventual inhabitants. Just as it had been determined that the best way to colonize Mars over the short term was to genetically modify the human genome so that future inhabitants would be more suitable for life on the red planet, so it was decided that Venusian colonists would be another new breed of humans. Thus the next branch of *Homo cosmos* was born. Dark-skinned, elfin, and exotically beautiful, aphrodites became Venus' proud native race, the wealthy and sophisticated denizens of the Evening Star.

From the beginning, the Venusian Socialist Republic was and always had been a loyal member of the Coalition. Although aphrodites tended to be arrogant and somewhat distrustful of reactionary capitalist terrans, they had never sided with the outer planets separatist movement. Earth and the Moon were their closest neighbors, while the Martian terraforming effort consumed most of the raw material generated by Venera Stratos, and it didn't pay to attack your best customers. So Starry Messenger had never gained much of a foothold on Venera Stratos or any of the other Venusian colonies. The group had taken its name from Venus' other planetary neighbor, but that didn't mean they were friends, let alone invited guests.

Which was why it seemed so unlikely that the Interplanetary Police Force would pick up rumors of a Starry Messenger plot to stage a terrorist attack against Venera Stratos. Yet Section Four, IPF's intelligence division, had learned from reliable informants that a previously unknown Starry Messenger cell was planning a major attack on Venera Stratos, and that it was believed to occur on March 12, 2305: Russian Day, a major Venusian holiday.

That's when the IPF decided to send in its troubleshooters. That's why Captain Future and the Futuremen had been dispatched to Venus.

IV

LIKE A METEOR, the recon pod streaked through Venus's upper atmosphere.

As the plasma shell around the tiny craft slowly faded, Curt saw the unblemished azure skies of Venus. Far below was a thick blanket of clouds the color of rotting citrus. A magnificent view, yet this was as close as he cared to come. Beneath the roiling cloud tops lay incendiary heat and a poisonous atmosphere that would crush the pod like a tin can, but not before he was roasted alive. So long as Curt remained above the clouds, he was safe.

"Skyhook rendezvous point Beta at bearing zero-point-seven degrees North by two-eight-five degrees West," Simon said, undistracted by the view. "Distance 27.3 nautical miles, over the visible horizon. Turn starboard thirty-one degrees and maintain present altitude. ETA five minutes, thirty-two seconds."

"Got it." Curt worked the control bars on either side of his seat, as the pod was shaken by the hurricane-force winds that prevailed even at this altitude. Until they reached the position where the skyhook would come down, he and the Brain would have to ride the violent westerly winds.

And that was only one of their difficulties.

"Scoopy's on the way down," Simon said. "We should see it any second now."

Curt peered through the window, squinting against the midday sun high overhead. He saw nothing for a few seconds. Then, just as the Brain predicted, a thin, vertical black line suddenly appeared at the farthest range of his vision. Materializing at the highest point in the sky, the narrow line was still too far away for him to make out any details, yet as he watched it slowly grew, stretching down from the zenith toward the clouds it would never touch.

This was the rotarvator's long end, the part that entered the Venusian atmosphere three times per orbit. Because Venera Stratos circled Venus in the same direction as the planet's axial rotation, with the tether revolving like the spokes of an immense wheel, from here it appeared as if Scoopy was slowly descending straight down from the heavens. Because its true angle of descent, though, was in the same direction as the prevailing westerlies, the tether was undisturbed by the high winds.

"Do you have a good fix on it?" Curt asked as he reached up to the overhead control panel.

"As well as our instruments allow, lad." There was a hint of pride in Simon's artificial voice. His interface with the pod was so intimate that it could be argued that he'd become part of the spacecraft itself; Curt's role as pilot was almost superfluous. "We're going to reach the receiving port at precisely the right time."

"Any local traffic?"

"Negative…nothing in our proximity, at least. A dirigible lifted off from Navka Planitia about an hour ago, but it's heading for rendezvous point Alpha and poses no problem for us. Ready to take over on your mark."

"All right then." Curt located a particular toggle switch above his head and rested his forefinger upon it. "Fantome field generation in three…two…one…mark."

He flicked the switch; an instant later, the view through the forward porthole went black, lightless and impenetrable. And for good reason; from hexagonal panels that unfolded themselves atop the pod, a light-and-radar deflecting energy bubble was enveloping the tiny craft. For all intents and purposes, the pod was now invisible; no one who might be aboard Scoopy would know that a space vehicle was on its way toward the receiving station.

In this way, Curt and Simon would be able to approach the sky city undetected, without Starry Messenger becoming aware of their presence. Indeed, no one on Venera Stratos knew what they were doing. In case Starry Messenger had infiltrated the colony's command center – something which had happened before on other SolCol installations – Captain Future was keeping secret the details of his plan. The aphrodites knew the Futuremen were coming…they just didn't know how.

The drawback was that Curt was effectively blind until the fantome generator was shut off, and the plan didn't call for them to do that until just before the pod docked with the receiving station. So he was depending on Simon to pilot the pod to its destination. The Brain would rely on his cybernetic interface with the pod's lidar, gravity sensors, and computers to give him precise, non-visual bearing. Instrument flying at its hairiest; an airplane pilot trying to make a runway landing in the midst of a raging snowstorm would have an easier time of it.

Simon must have realized from Curt's abrupt silence that he was nervous. "Relax, my boy," he said. "We'll be there before you know it."

"Okay. Sure." Stretching out his legs as much as he could, Curt idly ran his fingers through his red hair. Until recently he kept it short and trim, but lately he'd grown it out a little, keeping it short on the front and sides while letting it get long enough in the back so that he could tie it into a short, neat ponytail.

Curt smiled. He hadn't worn his hair this way since he was a kid: a teenager, really. That was around the time he made his first trip to Venus, the first time he set foot on Venera Stratos. When he met…

In the few inactive moments he had to himself while Simon piloted them in, Curt let memory take him back. Back here, but in the past.

It was a good memory. But it had barbs.

V

*T*HEN*...*

Curt didn't really want to visit Venus. Mars was a much more interesting planet, or at least that was the impression he got from his studies. And he would have loved to go to Earth again, even if doing so meant weeks of intense physical training to get his body reacclimatized to its higher gravity.

But Simon insisted that Venus should come first. It was closer, with a sidereal period which meant that it was easier to travel to from the Moon. And aphrodite *haute culture* was admired throughout the system, although that was largely a matter of taste; so far as Curt was concerned, no one had come up with anything half as entertaining as *The Adventures of Sarge Saturn*. So Venus was his destination, whether he liked it or not.

Yet as the beamship *Otis Adelbert Kline* completed its deceleration maneuvers and commenced final approach to Venera Stratos, Curt couldn't help but admit that the colony was one of the most impressive things his young eyes had ever seen. Yes, it was one of the largest spacehabs in the system; he knew that already. But it's one thing to read about it on your pad, and another to see it for yourself.

Curt let out a long, low whistle. Verbal gestures like that were something he'd lately picked up from old twentieth century vids. Whistling looked like fun, so he'd practiced doing it until he got it right. But it annoyed Otho. Sitting beside him in their small cabin, he gave his young companion an admonishing glare.

"Cut it out," he said, firm but not unkind.

Curt looked over at him. "Why can't I whistle?"

"You don't want to draw attention to yourself. Whistling does that."

"Aw, c'mon. Everyone whistles. It's easy...see?" Curt pursed his lips and blew the first notes of "The Lonely Spaceman," his favorite song. "Here, let's see you do it."

Otho scowled and looked away. He was still taller than Curt, but that would soon change; Curt was a teenager who'd eventually become an adult, whereas Otho would never change in appearance. He would always be as pale as an albino except for his emerald-green eyes, always have no hair anywhere on his body, and always be the same height and weight. Curt would grow older, but the android who was his de facto half-brother and lifelong companion never would age.

Or learn to whistle. Curt learned long ago that there were some things Otho was never able to do, and this was one of them.

"He means it, Curtis, and so do I." Simon Wright floated behind them, impellers purring softly. "It's all right if you do that when you're by yourself, but you need to be careful about how you behave in public. The aphrodites are a reserved people."

"Venusians, you mean."

"They prefer 'aphrodite.' 'Venusian' is the word you use to describe things that are part of Venus, but not its inhabitants."

"Sure thing, Brain. I understand." Curt gave Otho a sidelong glance as he said this, and the faintest of smiles appeared on the android's colorless face. It hadn't been but a few years ago that Otho, in a moment of disrespect, had given Simon this nickname. Along with Curt's late parents, Simon was Otho's co-creator, but he could be a trifle overbearing at times.

A fuzzy sound from Simon's vocoder, the equivalent of a sigh. "'Dr. Wright' or 'Simon' will do just fine, lad, but you already know that. No matter. We should be prepared to disembark as soon as the ferry arrives. It'll be easier if you and Otho pack while we still have gravity." His eyestalks twitched in Otho's direction as he spoke, a nonverbal cue.

"Got it." Planting his stikshoes against the carpeted deck, Otho stood up and pushed the button on the adjacent bulkhead that collapsed the chair back into the wall. "C'mon," he said to Curt. "We'll be docking in about fifteen minutes."

Curt quietly nodded as he got up to put away his own seat. Although the Brain had sprung for First Class accommodations, nothing changed the fact that a cabin for two aboard a beamship had precious little space, with everything designed to fold up and disappear when not in use. And while Otho's clothes were already packed, the things Curt had worn over the last three days were strewn about the floor and his still open bunk.

Sighing, Curt bent over to pick up the shirt he'd worn yesterday. As he did, he couldn't help but glance through the porthole. Venera Stratos was gradually becoming larger; he could already see the elongated inside-out terrain through the windows. People often called the Venusian colony one of the miracles of the twenty-third century, but even a miracle couldn't save him from the way he was feeling just then.

Curt Newton was fifteen years old. And he was bored with life.

VI

CURT WAS BORN ON EARTH, but while still an infant, his parents fled the comforts of the New Montauk oceanarc for the airless desolation of the Moon. Roger and Elaine Newton had done so to continue their efforts to create the first artificial person without interference from Victor Corvo, the billionaire venture capitalist who'd underwritten their research. The Newtons had learned that Corvo intended to use their orthogenic transhuman organism – or "otho" – as the prototype for an army of post-human soldiers, and meant to kill the husband and wife team behind it at the first opportunity. To avoid this fate, they decided to take over an abandoned laboratory beneath Tycho Crater and, once they'd faked their deaths in a space accident, secretly continue their research there.

The Newton family were accompanied by Simon Wright, their teacher and collaborator. Simon was dying from a rare form of cancer, and it was Roger and Elaine's intention to scan Simon's brain and transfer his consciousness into the otho's body once it was developed in the experimental bioclast they'd built.

But no plan survives contact with reality. Although Simon's brain was successfully transplanted into a specially-adapted robot drone, the android proved to be unsuitable for cerebral transfer, leaving Dr. Wright alive but no longer recognizably human. And no sooner had this occurred than something worse happened: Victor Corvo found them. The billionaire had seen through the ruse and tracked the refugees to their Tycho hideaway. Upon confirming that Roger and Elaine Newton were still alive, Corvo had his assassins murder the two scientists before planting a bomb that destroyed the lab.

Or so he believed. In actuality, Corvo destroyed only that part of the lab visible on the lunar surface. He completely missed the larger part twelve feet underground, including the living quarters where Simon had been left to mind Curt while his friends went above to confront Corvo.

With Roger and Elaine dead, Simon was left with an orphaned toddler to raise. Fortunately, he didn't have to do this alone. The experimental android – whom Roger and Elaine had naturally decided to name Otho – was ready to come out of the bioclast with not only a full-grown adult body but also a mind that could be educated far more quickly than Curt's. And they had an unexpected assistant: Grag, one of the robots that had refurbished Tycho Base.

But Victor Corvo was still out there, and Simon had little doubt that he wouldn't hesitate to kill the child of Roger and Elaine Newton if the billionaire – who'd since entered politics and become the Solar Coalition senator from the Lunar Republic – knew that he was still alive. So Curt was raised in secrecy deep beneath the lunar surface, with Simon Wright, Otho, and Grag as his only companions.

Although Curt was as bright as his parents and gifted with an innate curiosity that, with sufficient encouragement, would make him a natural scientist, Simon had lately observed that his isolation was threatening his mental and emotional stability. He'd gone through a childhood phase in which he'd invented a fantasy persona for himself, and although he eventually outgrew running around Tycho fighting imaginary villains, the fact remained that he'd met only a handful of people in his entire life, mainly during brief excursions to lunar settlements under Otho's close supervision. As reluctant as he was to expose Curt to the outside world, Simon knew that he couldn't keep him hidden forever.

The trip to Venus was only the second time they'd left the Moon. The first was a visit to Earth, and even then Simon made sure that Curt stayed away from major cities. And they didn't use Roger Newton's old racing yacht, the *Cornet*. The little teardrop-shaped craft had survived the faked explosion; since then, Simon and Otho had taken the precaution of rechristening it the *Comet* with the simple trick of changing the "r" and "n" on the ship's hull to an "m," but Simon decided to use commercial transportation instead, thereby making sure no one would recognize the *Comet* as a spacecraft presumed destroyed years ago. He used Tycho's shielded comlink to book a cabin aboard the weekly passenger liner from the Moon to Venus, and now…

VII

AND NOW, HERE THEY WERE, standing in line at Venera Stratos customs, waiting their turn to pass through the scanner arch.

The tattoo on the back of Curt's left hand identified him as Rab Cain, a terran originally from Manhattan Province, North America, currently a resident of Port Kepler, Lunar Republic. Otho was standing in front of him. As Curt watched, a green light flashed on above the arch, which was ornately fashioned with roses and cherubs to resemble a Greek proscenium.

Otho walked into the arch and, under the watchful eye of an aphrodite customs official seated in a nearby booth, handed over his passport folder and held up his left hand. His tattoo identified him as Vol Cotto, a selenite resident of Port Kepler and Rab Cain's legal guardian. An old freighter captain's cap cocked at a side angle helped affirm his disguise as an itinerant spacer. Many native-born selenites were as pale as Otho, so Vol Cotto's appearance didn't raise attention, nor did the arch detect any firearms or other weapons, the possession of which by private citizens was expressly prohibited by the Venusian Socialist Republic. The tattoo was as perfect as a fraud could be; the bored customs officer inside the booth checked Otho's passport and visa – which were just as phony and just as impeccable – waved him through, then nodded to Curt.

Curt did his best to hide his nervousness, but it scarcely mattered. His identity as Rab Cain was impeccable and the customs officer had no idea that the teenage boy who'd just walked through the arch was presumed to have perished fifteen years earlier. The official gave Curt's passport and visa little more than a glance. Otho was waiting for him on the other side.

"Nice job," he murmured. "Maybe you should be a smuggler."

Curt didn't respond. He disliked having to travel under an alias. "Couldn't you have come up with something better than Rab?" he asked as they walked over to baggage claim. "I really hate that stupid name."

"Sure." Otho winked at him. "How about Captain Future?"

Curt scowled. Otho had never let him live down the name he'd given his childhood make-believe character. Noticing his expression, Otho gave him a light punch in the arm. "C'mon, take it easy…it's a joke."

"Ha. Ha."

By then, they'd reached the baggage claim area where their belongings awaited pickup. Simon hovered nearby, along with a couple of robots belonging to other First Class passengers. "Good afternoon, Master Rab," he said, publicly pretending to be a simple-minded automaton. "Shall I carry your bags for you?"

This couldn't help but force a laugh out of Curt. For the time being, while they were in public, Simon was pretending to be nothing more what he appeared to be: a robotic drone, the sort of thing a spoiled young man might have as his servant. "Certainly, Brain. Make sure you don't drop them."

"I shall endeavor to serve you well." There was an edge to Simon's voice as his claws dipped to pick up the two flight bags Curt had brought. Otho smiled as he hoisted his own bag.

Looking about, Curt happened to notice one of the 'bots silently standing beside them. He did a double-take; it was a 200-series Grag, nearly identical to the companion they'd left behind on the Moon. But that Grag, while superficially similar to the countless other robots that came off an assembly line in Indiana, was a different creature entirely, possessing intelligence and even emerging empathy superior to other 'bots of its type. Elaine Newton had theorized that Grag – who'd taken its manufacturer's name as its own – was a product of AI evolution, a heuristic development unplanned by its human designers.

This Grag wasn't that Grag, who was guarding Tycho Base while Curt, Simon, and Otho were away. Seeing the silent 'bot, Curt found himself missing his strong, silent friend. At least Grag didn't constantly treat him like a child…

"Let's go. You don't want to hang around here all day." Otho was already walking away, Simon purring along beside him. "I want to see what the rest of this place looks like."

"Yeah…coming." A last glance at the anonymous 'bot, then Curt hastened to catch up. As they followed the signs to the nearby tram station, though, he couldn't help but wish that they'd stayed on the Moon. He'd just arrived, and already he was tired of Venus.

This was going to be a rotten trip.

VIII

HIS OPINION SOFTENED a bit once they reached the Hotel Venera, From the balcony of their third-floor suite, Curt gazed in awe at the colony. He'd seen pictures of the interior of Venera Stratos, even taken a virtual tour while aboard the *Kline, y*et nothing could prepare him for the real thing.

Past the hotel gardens and swimming pool, the town of Karpovgrad stretched out before him, its narrow streets, stucco walls, and tile roofs giving it a vaguely Spanish appearance. But the town's resemblance to anything Earth-like came to end with a black trench, a hundred yards wide, that stretched north and south across the equator as far as the eye could see. Sunlight streaming through the trench revealed that it was an immense window; as the colony orbited Venus, the window would gradually darken, with night falling on the enclosed world within.

The landscape continued on the other side of the window. Instead of disappearing over the horizon, though, it gradually sloped upward, its park-like trees, ponds, and bike paths apparently defying gravity. Up and up and up rose the concave far wall, its features diminishing but never disappearing except behind filmy clouds. Craning his neck, Curt looked straight up. Directly above him was another town much like Karpovgrad, upside-down and 1,600 feet above his head.

Vertigo clutched at his stomach. He hastily looked down before he became sick. It would take a while to get used to this. On the other hand, they were going to be here only a week, so by the time he did, they'd be ready to go home.

Back to hiding beneath a lunar crater with a cyborg, a 'bot, and an android as his only companions. Suddenly, for all of its uncomfortable strangeness, Curt found himself wanting to see as much of Venera Stratos as he could, if only because it was different. And that was the idea, except...

–Curt? Are you listening?

Simon's voice came to him through the augmented neural net implant within his cerebellum. Like most people, Curt's Anni had been nanosurgically introduced to his brain shortly after he was born. Unlike others, though, Curt wasn't dependent on public Anni nodes for communications or data retrieval. The ring on his left hand – a clear jewel in a gold crown, capable of projecting a holographic image of the solar system – was his own private node. He'd inherited the ring from his father, but it wasn't until just recently that the Brain had finally decided to entrust it to him.

—Yes, Simon, he thought. *I'm out on the balcony.* Curt peered over his shoulder. Through the balcony's sliding glass door, he saw Otho. The android was sprawled on a sofa, back turned to him, idly watching a Beethoven McGee concert on the holo. The Brain was nowhere in sight. *– Where are you?*

—Outside. Checking the hotel grounds. I can see you…look down.

Curt looked down from the balcony. It took a moment to spot Simon. He was floating among the hibiscuses surrounding the swimming terrace, unnoticed by the handful of hotel guests lounging poolside. No wonder; he was indistinguishable from any of the innumerable service 'bots they'd seen since their arrival.

Curt almost asked what the Brain was looking for, but didn't. He didn't need to. Whenever they traveled outside Tycho, Curt's safety was Simon's first concern. It was as if he expected there to be wanted posters all over the system: Reward! For Curt Newton – Presumed Dead for the Last Fifteen Years, But We Can't Be Too Sure.

Simon's eyestalks moved as he regarded Curt from the distance. *– You need to be careful about exposing yourself.*

"I'm exposing myself?" In mock horror, Curt hastily glanced down at the front of his trousers, checking his fly. "Nope, I'm okay…thanks for reminding me, though."

The Brain was not amused. *– This is not a joke, Curtis. We must always be cognizant of the fact that there are those who'd want to know that Roger and Elaine Newton's only child is still alive.*

"Yeah, I'm sure they lose sleep over that."

—Regardless of whether you take this seriously, I'll remind you again of the rules. While we're here, your name is Rab Cain. Other than that, it's nobody's business who you are or where you're from. You're to avoid speaking to anyone, and if you do, you're to say as little to them as you can. Understand?"

Curt rolled his eyes. He'd heard this many times before. "Understood."

—Above all, you are never to go anywhere without either Otho or me. You are never to go any place without one of us accompanying you, or at the very least without our express permission. Do you understand that, too?

This time, Curt did not answer at once. Instead, he stared down at the cyborg hovering among the small, flowering shrubs. It was fortunate that the virtual telepathy afforded by his Anni wasn't capable of conveying emotion as well as conscious thoughts; otherwise Simon would be horrified to know how the son of his deceased friends felt about him just then.

"I'm not a child," Curt said.

–Do you understand? Simon insisted.

"I understand."

–Very well. For the rest of the day and tonight, we'll rest from our travels. Tomorrow morning, we'll begin our tour of Venera Stratos, beginning with the history museum. Here is our tentative schedule…

As the Brain commenced a recital of their itinerary for the next several days, he floated away from the pool. By then, Curt noticed shadows beginning to lengthen along this side of the colony. Venera Stratos' orbit was taking it around Venus's night side. Curt observed the coming twilight with newfound interest. He wondered just how dark it would get here, without the presence of the earthlight he'd grown up expecting during the long lunar nights of the Moon.

Dark enough to hide in?

He shook his head. Running away was out of the question. For one thing, he wouldn't get far. Simon would figure out where he'd gone – he wasn't nicknamed the Brain for nothing – and Otho wouldn't rest until he found Curt. After they returned to the Moon, they'd literally stick him where the sun wouldn't shine, in Tycho Base's caverns ten feet beneath the lunar surface. Then, he'd have to beg for another chance to leave home.

Still…a tempting thought.

IX

TWO DAYS LATER, HE MET THE GIRL.

It soon became clear that Simon Wright didn't have relaxation in mind when he'd planned the trip. He'd scheduled every day in advance, with Curt waking up early, having his meals at precise intervals, resting only on occasion, and going to sleep late. The Brain explained that it was important for Curt to learn as much as he could about Venus and the aphrodite colony in the week they would be spending on Venera Stratos. There would be little chance for a leisurely stroll through the park or sitting in a cloistered garden to contemplate abstract sculptures. Curt was there to learn, not have a vacation.

The trip to the history museum was only the first activity of the day. They spent the morning in its exhibit halls, with Curt receiving a nonstop lecture from Simon on the history of Venusian exploration and settlement. A quick lunch at the museum restaurant, then they boarded a tram and rode it to Venera Stratos' eastern end, where they joined a tour of the ore refinery sphere that was the colony's industrial base. This was barely over when they reboarded the tram that brought them back down to the main habitat.

At the Karpovgrad tram station, Simon insisted upon heading over to the edge of the nearby window to observe its thick, micrometeorite-proof panes being mopped and polished by a mixed-race cleaning crew of terrans, selenites, and aresians, the sort of menial labor apparently beneath the dignity of aphrodites. Curt wanted to step out onto the window, but discovered that this was against the law for anyone except custodians.

Returning to the hotel, he and Otho had dinner in the café – vegan, of course; aphrodites were not meat-eaters – before heading back to their suite. Simon was already there. He handed Curt a slate loaded with the evening's tutorials, then settled on the living room floor next to a wall outlet to recharge his batteries. Otho sat on the couch and watched a space op on the holo. Alone in his room, Curt studied until he dozed off with the slate on his chest.

The following morning, they started again.

Between walking tours and seemingly endless discourses on local history, customs, and industry, Curt had only brief encounters with the aphrodites themselves. Among the bio-engineered *Homo cosmos* races of the solar system, the native Venusians were exotic beyond compare: ebony skin, white hair, tall and elfin-faced. Yet they were also aloof and proud, stoical in expression and taciturn in word, never rude but seldom welcoming. From the condescending way everyone from hotel staff to tour guides spoke to Curt and his companions, it was clear that Venera Stratos' residents regarded offworld visitors as philistines incapable of fully appreciating the renaissance society the colonists had created over the three generations the spacehab had been in existence.

Early in the afternoon of the second day, Curt, Otho, and Simon were on Strugatski campus of Tsiolkovsky University, spending the day at a public seminar on the commercial applications of Venusian vulcanology. At one point, sitting in a lecture hall and listening to a geologist hold forth on the highlands of the Lloroma Planitia, Curt caught himself nodding off. Otho noticed this, and although Simon insisted on remaining – "How can you leave? This is absolutely fascinating!" – he grudgingly allowed Curt a chance to take a break.

With Otho as his chaperone, Curt left the hall and strolled a short distance off campus, where they found an ornate fountain in the middle of the town square. Aphrodites strolled about, many of them students around Curt's age. There was a vendor selling refreshments from a pushcart; they each bought a sorbet, then went over to the fountain and sat down on the rounded edge of its tub where they could feel the cool mist at their backs.

"So what do you think of this place?" Otho asked.

Curt looked about. The square wasn't all that much different than any other place they'd yet visited. "It's nice. I like the fountain."

"Venus, I mean. Are you enjoying the trip?"

Curt said nothing for a moment. He dug his spoon into the paper cup and the lump of raspberry sorbet it held. "It's okay," he said at last.

"'It's okay.'" Otho repeated what Curt had just said with only a trace of mimicry. "My, such enthusiasm –"

"I said it's okay, didn't I?"

Otho lifted his cat-like green eyes toward the populated ceiling far above, calmly regarding the tiny sailboats on the small lake directly overhead. "Yes, you did," he said after a moment, "but I don't think you mean it. Not that I blame you. I told Brain that a seminar might be a bit much –"

"Oh no, not at all." Curt didn't look at him. "It's absolutely riveting. I can't thank you enough for bringing me."

"I'll tell Simon you said that. I'm sure he'll be pleased. C'mon…what's bothering you?"

Curt knew what he wanted to say, but was having a hard time finding a way to say it that wouldn't make Otho angry or hurt his feelings. He was still searching for words when he happened to look up again, and that's when he saw her.

There was a girl sitting on the fountain, on the other side of Otho just a few yards. Because the tub's edge was rounded, she was seated so that Curt could see her even though he appeared to be looking at Otho instead. She was an aphrodite, yet her lighter skin and dark brown hair hinted at multiracial ancestry. In any case, she appeared to be about Curt's age. She was pretty – no, more than pretty: she was beautiful – and she was looking straight at him.

The quiet, knowing smile on her face hinted that she'd overheard everything and had come up with an answer of her own. Then a soft voice, feminine and undoubtedly hers, whispered to him through his Anni:

–Tell him the truth.

The girl was speaking to him. He didn't know how she'd managed to access his Anni, but apparently she knew a trick or two. However she'd done this, what she said made sense.

"I'm bored," Curt said. "I'm bored and –" he hesitated "– I want you to leave me alone."

"You want me to do **what**?" Otho stared at him

Smiling, the girl nodded ever so slightly. *–Go on.*

"I want you and the Brain to leave me alone." Curt felt his face becoming warm, his heart beating against his chest. "You…you two have been on my back the whole time we've been here. I can't so much as go to the bathroom without one of you shadowing me, and I'm really sick of –"

"Curt, what's come over you?" Otho's slanted green eyes were bewildered. "You know the rules. Your safety, your security, is the most important thing. You can't just –"

"Really? Is that what you think?" Letting the sorbet fall to the pavement, Curt abruptly stood up. "Hey, everyone!" he yelled, waving hands back and forth above his head. "I'm Curt Newton! You hear? **Curt Newton!** I'm –!"

"Stop it!" Otho grabbed him by the front of his shirt and tried to haul him back to where he'd been sitting. Curt tugged himself free, causing Otho to anxiously look about. "What are you trying to do, draw attention to yourself?"

"Yeah, and so what?" Curt gestured to the passers-by around them, who'd only given him curious or annoyed glances before going back to what they'd been doing. "Look…nobody cares! They have no idea who I am, and I don't think they'd give a damn even if they did! This whole pretense is pointless!"

The girl was the only person who seemed to have noticed Curt's outburst. Her smile was replaced by a quizzical expression, as if what he'd just said had raised a question in her own mind. But she didn't say anything to him.

Noticing the direction in which Curt kept glancing, Otho peered over his shoulder at her. The girl looked away before their eyes could meet, but as soon as Otho turned away again, she caught Curt's attention once more…

No words. But this time, she winked at him.

She **winked** at him!

Curt almost laughed out loud. If she'd blown him a kiss, he wouldn't have been more surprised. Or delighted.

"It's…this isn't like you." Otho still hadn't seen her. He shook his head, bewildered by Curt's obstinacy. "I don't think you should go back to the seminar –"

"Oh, please…don't break my heart!" Curt was unable to keep the sarcasm from his voice. "I don't know if I can get through the day, deprived of knowing the role violent volcanic episodes have had in reshaping the Venusian terrain during the –"

"That's enough." Otho stood up. "We're going back to the hotel."

"Ah, yes…the good old Hotel Venera." Curt deliberately avoided looking at the girl, but he spoke just loud enough so that she couldn't miss what he said. "I can't wait to get back to my view from the third-floor balcony. I can watch people in the pool and everything."

Otho didn't notice, but the girl did. She nodded and smiled.

– Message received and understood. See you tonight.

She then stood up and sauntered away. As Curt angrily shook off the hand Otho attempted to put on his arm, he hoped like he'd never hoped for anything before that she'd keep her promise.

And she did.

X

THAT EVENING, CURT DID HIS BEST to pretend that nothing was different. When the Brain returned to the hotel, he found Curt on the living room couch, watching *Sarge Saturn* on the holo. Otho took Simon out on the balcony and told him about the argument. As soon as the two of them came back in, Curt muted the kidvid and went about making apologies.

It was harder than he thought it would be. This wasn't the first time he'd talked back to Otho or walked out on Simon; nonetheless, his insubordination had taken them by surprise. It didn't help that Curt's apologies sounded insincere even to himself; all three of them knew that he didn't really mean it when he said that he'd been wrong and that he shouldn't have acted that way. Neither Otho nor Simon were willing to call him on it, though, and even false contrition is better than none at all. So they took him at his word. They didn't have much choice.

Afterwards, Otho and Curt had dinner together in silence, and once the Brain downloaded the evening tutorial into his slate, Curt went to his room and closed the door behind him. Sitting on the bed, slate propped against his knees, Curt tried to absorb the text he'd been assigned, only to find his attention wandering. His gaze kept traveling to the sliding glass doors beside his bed. His room had its own balcony door; he'd come to enjoy the luxury of leaving it open to let in the night air, something he couldn't do on the Moon.

Would she come? If so, how? Or was she expecting him to come to her? He decided to wait and see whether she'd show up, hoping he hadn't misunderstood her.

The hours crawled by. From the other side of the wall, he could hear the faint sound of the holo: Otho and the Brain were watching some vidrama, which was as sophisticated and stultifying as just about all aphroditean performance art was. After a while, he heard the holo go silent. Curt fixed his gaze upon the pad before him. A few moments later, the bedroom door opened and Otho peered in.

"Still studying?" he asked. Curt barely glanced at him as he nodded. "Don't stay up too late. We've got another full day tomorrow."

Curt quietly nodded again. Otho seemed to want to say something more, but he didn't. Instead, he closed the door without another word.

A few more minutes passed. Then, the light behind the space beneath the bedroom door went out, and he heard the door to Otho's room open and shut. Simon would still be in the living room, but not completely awake, although the Brain no longer slept in the normal sense of the word, once a day he'd come to a rest near an outlet, plug in his cyborg body for a battery recharge, lower his eyestalks, and allow himself to drift off into a semiconscious state much like dream-sleep.

Curt was still wondering how much longer he should wait before he crept out onto the balcony when he heard a faint sound from outside. Putting the pad aside, he sat up on the bed and looked out to see a thin black rope drop to the balcony floor from somewhere above. The rope jerked back and forth a few times, then a pair of legs came into sight.

And then the girl was there.

There was something almost magical about the way she descended, like she was performing the fabled Indian rope trick, only in reverse. She wore a black, skin-tight bodysuit with a matching cape slung over her shoulders, its hood raised above her head. She looked like a shadow come to life, and she moved like one, too. The soles of her black slippers touched the balcony soundlessly, and her cape settled about her with nothing more than the faint rustle of a night bird's wing.

Smiling, she raised a gloved hand and beckoned him with crooked finger. As quietly as possible, Curt got up and tip-toed out onto the balcony. A wary glance at the other windows told him that Otho and the Brain were still asleep, or at least unaware that they were being visited…or so he hoped. Looking up, Curt let his gaze travel up the dangling rope. It disappeared somewhere past the roof eaves.

"How did you –?" he started to whisper.

The girl hastily stepped forward to place a finger against his lips. Suddenly, he understood why: it was possible that Simon or Otho might be eavesdropping, either through his Anni or by simply listening from outside his room. Instead, she moved closer, bringing her face so close to his that he felt her soft lips brush lightly against his cheek. She was nearly as tall as he, he was startled to realize.

"One question," she asked, so softly that someone standing next to them wouldn't have heard her. "Do you want to get away from here?"

Somehow, the whisper in his ear felt more intimate than a voice in his mind. Curt didn't have to contemplate this mystery for very long. He nodded. "Can you climb?" she asked. Curt unhesitatingly nodded again.

"Good." Stepping back, she grasped the rope and tugged on it a couple of times to make sure that it was still secure. "You go first. Wait for me at the top."

She didn't warn him to be quiet because she didn't need to, but there was an unspoken challenge in her whispered voice. Nor did she need to tell him that if he couldn't or wouldn't come with her, this would be the last he'd see of her. No second chances.

Curt took hold of the rope. He stopped to look at the other windows one more time, then he grasped the rope tightly in his hands and…no, wait. One more thing. Letting go of the rope, he raised his left hand and tugged the ring from his middle finger.

Curt wanted to leave it behind not only because it was an irreplaceable heirloom, but also because its Anni link would allow Otho and Simon to find him if they discovered that he was missing. Reaching in through the open balcony door, he tossed the ring on the bed. Then he quietly slid the door shut, grasped the rope again, and began to climb.

Since childhood, Simon and Otho had put Curt through a two-hour exercise regimen every sol that included everything from basic calisthenics to the martial arts. Gymnastics hadn't been neglected, and although Tycho Base's small gym didn't include a climbing rope – its ceiling was too low – Otho had compensated by teaching him the fundamentals of rock-climbing on the crater walls. So Curt had no trouble shimmying up the girl's rope. It helped that it had been knotted every couple of feet; nonetheless, he could feel her eyes on him as he climbed upwards, observing his progress as if to make sure he could do as he claimed.

He'd scarcely reached the sloping tile roof when the girl mounted the rope herself. Balancing himself on his haunches, Curt watched as she swiftly made the return climb. Now he realized the purpose of the hooded cape:; it effectively hid her from anyone who might have glanced up from the garden below.

A quick downward glance to see if they'd been spotted, then she tapped him on the arm and pointed toward the crest of the roof. He nodded, crouching on his hips and toes, and followed her up the roof. She paused to untie her rope from the support legs of a rain cistern and wrap it into a coil, then she led him to the top of a fire tower rising along one side of the building.

Although the way down was easy, she took her time, making sure each step they took was in darkness and silence. They didn't speak to each other until they'd stolen through the tree-shrouded courtyard and were on the other side of the terra cotta wall surrounding it. It wasn't until then that she let them stop and catch their breaths.

"You're very good," she said softly as she lowered her hood and looked at him, her dark eyes shining in the light of a cast-iron lamp atop the wall. "You climbed that rope like a thief."

"Is that what you are?" Curt kept his voice as low as hers. "A thief, I mean."

The girl didn't reply. She looked away, checking the cobblestone street below to ascertain that they were alone. "I'll make you a deal," she said at last. "I'll tell you no lies if you agree to tell me none, and we don't answer questions if we don't want to. Fair enough?"

He thought it over for a second, then nodded. "All right. Fair enough. Can I ask your name?"

"Ashi Lenyr. And yours?"

"Rab Cain," he replied, then immediately shook his head. "No, that's not true. It's Curt…Curt Newton."

"I know…you shouted it in the middle of University Square, remember?" Ashi seemed satisfied by his response. "Thanks for not lying," she added, and Curt realized that he'd just passed another test. "All right, Curt," she went on, "let me ask you something else. Did you mean what you said to your friend the other day about being bored and tired of having them shadow you all the time?"

"Yes. Yes, I did. But what –?"

"Then come with me," Ashi said, "and I'll show you things you've never seen before."

Curt hesitated, then nodded again. Once more, Ashi darted a look up and down the street. Then she took him by the hand, and together they fled into the warm darkness.

XI

Every night should be so beautiful. Every night should be so mysterious.

Venera Stratos wrapped itself around the boy and the girl like a barrel of fireflies. Some distance from the hotel, Ashi led Curt into a small park and paused to let him look up in awestruck wonder. Everywhere his eyes turned, he saw tiny lights of every color imaginable. Houses, street lamps, walkways, shops, and vehicles arched above his head as an immense ceiling dome, more spectacular than even the Moon's night sky. When he looked straight ahead or straight behind toward the spacehab's western and eastern ends, the lights slowly revolved in vertiginous majesty, unsettling yet wonderful.

His knees weakened and he felt as if he was about to fall, then a pair of tender but sturdy hands grasped his shoulders. "Steady," Ashi murmured. "It's only an illusion. Look at something else."

Curt let his gaze fall to her. Ashi Lenyr stood before him, half-visible in the illumination of the walkway lights. Her face was shadowed by the cape's hood, but he could make out a smile nonetheless. Seeing her world through his eyes, she was sharing his sense of wonder.

"This is…so incredible." It was all he could manage to say.

A quiet chuckle. "Well, as they say on Earth –" a passable imitation of an old-style New York accent "– baby, you ain't seen nuthin' yet."

Curt laughed at this, and suddenly the vertigo went away, to be replaced by…he didn't know what it was, but it was something he'd never felt before. The world was lovely and amazing, but the most lovely and amazing part of it was the girl who stood in front of him. All of a sudden, he had the impulse to lean forward and kiss her.

As he stepped closer, though, she withdrew just the same distance. "C'mon, we need to get out of here." She glanced past him, in the direction they'd just come. "Your friends might have figured out that you've taken off. If they're following us or they've called the proctors, I don't want to get caught…do you?"

Ashi settled the issue by taking him by the hand. Somewhere along the line, she'd removed her gloves. Her touch was warm. In that moment, any lingering reluctance Curt may have had about running off with her vanished.

"No, I don't," he said. "Where do you want to go?"

"This way." And then she dropped his hand, turned about, and began to jog down the walkway, heading toward a nearby trellis gate.

Curt followed her. Beauty must be pursued.

XII

Not far from the park, in a narrow alley between two shops, Ashi Lenyr located what appeared to be a manhole, an iron hatchcover set within the cobblestone pavement. Like everything else in the colony, it was a piece of art; its ironwork featured a bas-relief Aquarius bearing a pitcher of water. She found a square cobblestone on the left side of the hatch, pried it open with her fingertips, and entered a six-digit code number on the keypad concealed beneath it. The hatch popped open with a hydraulic hiss, allowing pale blue light to escape. Below was a ladder leading down a four-foot shaft.

Ashi silently gestured for Curt to climb down; she followed him, pausing at the top of the ladder to close the hatch behind them. Below the manhole lay the cross-shaped intersection of two narrow tunnels, metal tubes leading away in four directions. Alphanumeric codes stenciled on unadorned metal walls designated their present location, or would have if Curt had understood what they meant.

"Service maze," Ashi said, keeping her voice low so that it wouldn't echo. "It runs under everything above us. It's how some of us get around." She paused. "And live," she added.

"Where's your home?"

"I just told you…down here." Her expression darkened and she looked away. "Or at least I do now."

"Why –?"

"Later." She turned to the left and began moving down the tunnel marked E212-S. Curt had a good sense of direction. Even underground, he determined that they were headed east, away from the hotel. He followed her, admiring the soundless way in which she walked. Her stealth was catlike, graceful and silent.

They traveled quietly, with Ashi stopping at each intersection to cautiously peer around the corner and see if anyone was around. This time of night, though, the maze appeared to be deserted. In some places, the tunnel hummed as if machinery worked on the other side of the closed sliding doors they occasionally passed. Every so often they came upon a 'bot of one sort or another, none of which noticed them but went about their errands with the single-minded intensity of programmed minds. Otherwise, the maze belonged to them, at least for a while; above their heads, the colony slept.

E212-S came to an abrupt end at a sphincter hatch marked EW14. Stenciled on the wall beside it was a warning:

Authorized Personnel ONLY Beyond This Point!
No Visitors Permitted!

Ashi reached to the keypad below the sign, then paused to look over her shoulder at him.

"All right," she whispered, "until now, all you've done wrong is a little minor trespassing. If someone catches you, it'll mean civil probation, maybe a fine. You're a tourist, though –"

"A visitor," Curt insisted. "I'm a visitor, not a tourist."

A wry smile. "If you get in trouble, better let them call you a tourist. You'll get off easy if the magistrates think you're just some stupid kid from Earth." The smile vanished. "But if you let me take you any further and you get caught…if **we** get caught…then it won't go down so easy. If you're lucky, the least they'll do is expel you and tell you never to come back. If you're not lucky –" she shrugged "–well, you'd be staying for a while longer, and not as a guest."

"Then why are you –?"

"Remember I said, 'You ain't seen nothin' yet?'" Ashi tapped a finger against the door. "This is what I'm talking about. You'll never see this any other way. At least not on a guided tour."

"Is it worth it?"

"It's worth it."

Curt hesitated, then nodded. Ashi entered a code into the keypad and the door irised open. Darkness lay on the other side. "Walk carefully," she whispered as she held out her hand to him, "and keep your voice down."

Curt took her hand and let her lead him through the door. It closed behind them. The surface beneath his shoes became slick, almost frictionless; it felt as if he was walking on ice. He could see nothing the first few steps he took, then his eyes adjusted to the gloom. Once again he saw the barrel of light that constituted Venera Stratos's night sky…but now, the lights were beneath his feet as well.

He looked down and saw stars.

Below him, constellations slowly moved through the black emptiness of space. That wasn't all. As he watched, it seemed as if the stars would reach a certain invisible line, then abruptly start moving back the direction from which they'd come, in the same perfect order. The vista stretched before him for many miles; it was as if he and Ashi were standing within a kaleidoscope, with stars slowly turning beneath their feet and in the sky above their heads. In the midnight hour, they'd come to a place both surreal and serene, where time itself no longer seemed to matter.

"We're standing on one of the windows," he said quietly.

"You figured it out." Ashi's laughter was so quiet, it could have been an angel's. "Only cleaning crews are allowed to come out here. We came through one of the access tunnels they use. Do you know it takes an entire year for them to clean each of the windows, and by the time they're through –?"

"It's time to start over again. Yeah, that's what I was told." Curt realized that the star-reversal effect was caused by the reflection of starlight upon the mirrors used to bring sunshine into the colony. "Must be a great job."

"It's actually pretty tedious." Still holding his hand, Ashi walked a few more steps away from the door; looking back, Curt saw what hadn't been obvious until now, that the windows were located below ground-level with the rest of the colony. That and the guardrail running alongside the window pane prevented people from doing what he and Ashi were doing now. "Boring as hell," she added. "Worst job I ever had."

That answered Curt's unspoken question of how she knew how to get into the maze and through the service doors. "I would've thought it would be a great job," he replied, and she gave him a sharp look. "I mean, you get to see this every day, and you're also performing a valuable public service."

"Are you joking?"

"No. Not at all. I mean, think of all the dust that must came from living in a closed environment like this. That and the humidity…well, it would be a big job to keep the windows clean, or everyone here would have a big problem."

"So someone has to clean up after everyone else, is that it?" Ashi dropped his hand. "And, of course, that's people like me –"

"What? I didn't say that!" Curt's voice began to rise, and the girl shushed him with an urgent hiss. "That's not what I'm saying at all," he went on, returning his voice to a whisper as he stepped closer to her again. "I'm just trying to say…just trying to –"

Ashi grabbed him by the shoulders, pulled Curt against herself, and kissed him.

It startled and even scared him. He knew what a kiss was, of course, but until this moment no one had ever done this to him…**with** him. But her mouth was soft and amazingly warm, her lips moved tenderly against his, her body was a firm, living thing that wrapped itself around him. The impulse to flee was gone in a second; his eyes closed of their own accord, and he let himself be taken by this lovely young lady of darkness and mystery.

Time returned, and it was only reluctantly that they broke apart from one another. Opening his eyes again, Curt found her regarding him with the same wry, knowing smile as before.

"Tell that was your first kiss," she whispered, and grinned when he nodded. "Thought so."

"Who are you?" He knew that was a question she was reluctant to answer, but he had to ask it anyway.

"I'll tell you," she said as she took him by the hand again, "but not here. C'mon, we've got to go before someone spots us."

Curt nodded. The chances she'd taken by bringing him out here were probably even greater than his own, and the longer they remained on the window, the higher the probability of being spotted by a proctor on night patrol. "Where are we going now?" he asked as he followed her back to the service door.

"Home. I'm taking you home."

XIII

IT TOOK A WHILE TO GET THERE – twice they had to elude security drones prowling the maze – but finally they reached the place that Ashi called home. It was a custodial closet amid one of the colony's freshwater reservoirs, a cubbyhole located between enormous tanks of burnished Venusian steel, disused and long since forgotten. Ashi had managed to reset the lock so it would accept a keypad code only she knew, and painted over the sign to make it just another anonymous door among thousands in the maze.

There wasn't much. She'd removed everything that had once been stored there, replacing it with her handful of belongings. A cot with a sleeping bag. An upended crate serving as a table, lit by an ostrich-neck lamp. A hot plate. A wire rack crammed with miscellany, from cookware to hair bands. Her clothes lay in piles here and there, the dirty ones indistinguishable from the clean. Water came from bottles and food from wrappers, both stored in a small refrigerator humming in the corner.

"In case you're wondering," Ashi said as Curt made a place for himself on the cot, "there's a restroom about fifty feet away, and when I need a shower I visit a locker room one of the custodians lets me use." Taking off her gloves, she held up her left hand, showing off the I.D. tattoo on the back of her wrist. "Fake. So long as no one disables it, I've got the run of the place."

"Unless you get caught," Curt said.

"Not going to happen." Ashi removed her cape. It was apparently her favorite garment, because she didn't drop it on the floor along with the leggings and sweaters and underwear heaped here and there, but instead carefully hung it on a coat hook behind the door. The black leotard she wore beneath it fit her like a second skin; she had a gymnast's body: small breasts, long torso, tight and muscular hips. The only part of her that seemed out of place were her feet, which somehow seemed too large for the soft-sole dancer's moccasins she wore.

It was hard for Curt to not stare at her. This was the first time he'd ever been alone with a girl. Life on the Moon had always been lonely, and the covert nature of his existence hadn't given him much opportunity to interact with people of other genders. When she turned toward him again, she seemed to notice the way he was regarding her, for she folded her arms protectively across her chest and stared back at him until he averted his gaze.

"Why do you live here?" he asked. "Don't you have...?"

His voice trailed off. He'd promised her that he wouldn't ask questions that she didn't want to answer, but he didn't know any other way to ask that which seemed most obvious. Yet she didn't seem to mind.

"I live here because I want to," Ashi replied. "You're right...I'm a thief." She sat down on the other end of the cot, settling her back against the wall behind her. "Just about everything here was stolen," she said, not bragging about it but not shying away from the truth either. "When I saw you yesterday, I was casing a shop near the university. Live the way I do, it's kinda hard to have a normal life, y'know what I mean?"

"No, I don't. Why do you steal? I thought the government takes care of everyone's needs."

"Sure it does." Bending forward, she opened the fridge and pulled out a couple of pints of water. "The Venusian Socialist Republic is dedicated to the rights, welfare, and happiness of all its citizens," she recited as she handed a bottle to Curt. "Unless, of course, you happen to be a citizen they really don't want...like me."

She was not a full-blooded aphrodite, she went on to explain. Although her mother was *Homo cosmos aphrodite,* born and raised on Venera Stratos, her father was baseline *Homo sapiens* from Earth, with light skin and dark hair. So their daughter was multiracial, which should have made no difference, but did. As Ashi grew older, she learned first-hand a central hypocrisy of Venera Stratos society: for all of its cultural refinement, there was also a thread of racism, the xenomorphic variety. Aphrodites liked to think of themselves as the most advanced branch of the tree of humanity, so they tended to have an unspoken dislike and distrust of anyone whose skin and eyes weren't sufficiently dark, whose hair wasn't silken and platinum-blond.

Ashi became an outcast early in life, her mother and father ostracized for being a mixed-race couple. Yet, when her parents finally made the decision to immigrate to Earth, she decided to remain. Venera Stratos was the only world she'd ever known; as tough as things were, she'd rather stay in the place where she'd been born and raised than try to make a new life on what amounted to an alien planet.

So, she ran away the night before her family was scheduled to depart from Venus. By then, it was too late for her parents to search long for her; they boarded the ship to Earth without her. She hadn't seen them since. At first, she scratched out a living above ground, living in a tiny apartment while working the sort of odd jobs left to those on the lowest rung of Venera Stratos society. People like her. Finally, she got fed up with being treated like **them** and decided to go rogue.

So, here she was: living on the fringes, stealing what she needed to get by. Ashi eventually became good enough to be a thief for hire, entering someone's home or workplace to purloin an object that another individual wanted to acquire. She'd spotted Curt while preparing for one such job; when he'd lost his temper at Otho, she recognized a kindred soul.

"But, I'm not a thief," Curt insisted.

"Didn't say you were." Ashi folded her legs beneath herself. "I heard you tell your friend that you're tired of pretending to be someone besides who you really are. I know how that is, and I know how lonely it can be…and don't tell me you aren't, because you confirmed that the moment you kissed me."

Curt's face became warm. "**You** kissed **me** –"

"Sure, and I could tell how much you hated it."

"I…I didn't say I –"

Awkwardly, he started to reach for her, but she surprised him by planting a hand against his chest. "No, let's not get started on something we might not stop," she said, gently pushing him back. "Maybe…well, we ought to get to know each other a little better before we –"

Now it was her turn to go red and fumble for words. "Get to know each other a little better," Curt finished.

They looked at each other, neither knowing what to say. It suddenly became obvious how nervous each of them were about the same thing. Then, they giggled self-consciously, and suddenly broke down in helpless, full-throated laughter.

In the end, Curt spent the night with her.

He slept on the other side of the room, curled up on a pile of her clothes, her robe as his blanket. Her clothes smelled like her, and it was almost as if he was in her arms.

XIV

CURT SHOULD'VE RETURNED to the hotel the following morning, but he didn't.

Neither Otho nor Simon were capable of becoming livid, but it wasn't hard to imagine their reactions once they discovered that his bedroom was empty. There would be serious questions once he came back, with scolding and punishment to follow.

But, what if he didn't return?

Finding him would be difficult. He'd removed his ring and left it behind; so as long as Curt didn't access Anni through a local node, the Brain wouldn't be able to track him that way. Not only that, but he was with a girl who'd long since learned how to keep the law at arm's length.

So why go back? He was sick and tired of his guardians and their over-protectiveness. And he was **really** sick and tired of being called by his childhood nickname. Maybe it was time for Captain Future to disappear for a little while and Curt Newton to go out on his own.

These were the thoughts that passed through his mind when he awoke in Ashi's room. His watch told him it was 0756 local time; somewhere above the ceiling, morning had broken, the spacehab's mirrors bringing a semblance of sunrise to the cylindrical world. Curt waited until the girl woke up, and as she put together a breakfast of granola, dried fruit, and juice boxes, he told her what he'd been thinking.

Ashi heard him out, then nodded her agreement. She didn't mind sharing her quarters with him so long as he behaved himself – Curt didn't have to ask what she meant by that – and agreed to do whatever she told him to do without question, even if it meant breaking the law. Once he was ready to go back, she would lead him as close to the Hotel Venera as she could without being seen, then they'd say their goodbyes and Curt would forget that he'd ever seen her…or at least pretend.

"And what if I don't want to go back?"

An offhand shrug. "You're going back," Ashi said, digging her hand into the granola bag they'd been sharing. "You just don't know when, that's all."

Curt wanted to believe that she was wrong.

The first order of business, after they'd each visited the toilet and Ashi had him turn his back while she changed clothes, was whether and how to alter Curt's appearance. She believed that Otho would alert the authorities as soon as he discovered that Curt was missing – Curt hadn't yet told her that the Brain wasn't the robotic drone he appeared to be – but Curt didn't think so. Simon Wright's greatest fear was having anyone discover that Rab Cain was actually a young man who'd been presumed dead fifteen years ago; a missing person investigation might lead to just such a revelation. So, they didn't have to worry much about his face appearing on every screen in Venera Stratos. Aside from Simon, who couldn't wander on his own in public, the only individual who'd be searching for him was Otho…or Vol Cotto, as Curt continued to call him.

As he explained this, there was a querying look in her eyes. She already knew that Curt was here under an assumed name – she'd learned that when he'd blown up at Otho – but she didn't know why, and he left out just enough detail to raise the obvious questions: who was he, and why was he here? But, she apparently recalled the promise she herself had insisted that they make, so she didn't push Curt to talk about things that she wanted to know.

Curt was tempted to reveal everything about his past, just as Ashi had opened up to him. But, he remembered the dictum that Simon had made him remember the first time they'd ever traveled: *I have no name, I have no home, and it's nobody's business who I am.* He'd violated the first part of that already. He might eventually go all the way and tell her the rest…but not just yet.

In the end, they decided not to do anything about his appearance other than give him a beret to cover his red hair. He didn't need much more than that. As it turned out, Ashi was an expert at the art of evasion.

Otho had spent years tutoring Curt in the martial arts, and each day he'd engaged in mock combat with Grag. But, neither of his companions, nor Simon, had taught him how to elude surveillance cameras, disable security systems, or hide in plain sight. Ashi Lenyr knew all this. Like a spy, she could sneak into supposedly secure areas, dodging both living and electronic sentries; like a shadow, she could disappear at a moment's notice, becoming invisible even in a crowd. No one had ever caught her, and she bragged that no one ever would.

Curt became her apprentice. He adopted her pattern of sleeping through the morning, waking up early in the afternoon, and emerging from the maze shortly after dark. On occasion, they'd come above ground at daytime, when Ashi would teach him the art of reconnoitering prospective targets during normal business hours without being noticed.

Even at her age, Ashi was thoroughly professional, supporting herself through assignments given to her by a so-called "broker" who, in turn, was hired by others to have certain items illegally acquired for them. She claimed she could steal anything as long as it wasn't too large for her to carry, but her specialty was jewelry. Venusian diamonds were prized throughout the system. More plentiful than those found on Earth, they were also more valuable, since they had to be extracted by robots from the planet's volcanic highlands and transported up to Stratos. Most were used for industrial purposes, but every now and then, a diamond would be found that, once cut and polished, would produce a stone that would make South African gems look cheap by comparison. These were quite expensive, and some collectors on Earth and Luna simply didn't want to pay the price. That was where thieves like Ashi came in.

Curt admired her skill, but he wasn't comfortable with the idea of becoming a thief himself. Larceny wasn't in his heart, nor did he share Ashi's desire to get even with Venera Stratos high society. She made it clear to him, though, that if he wanted to remain with her, he couldn't keep his hands clean.

For the time being, he'd remain her student. Until he learned the craft, Curt wouldn't touch the jewels himself, but instead would act as her lookout while she was pulling a heist. Once she learned to trust him, she said, she'd let him come along while she made the drop at a specified location for later pickup by some individual working for her broker.

They lived by stealing food from restaurant kitchens and the homes of the wealthy. While more risky, Ashi seemed to particularly enjoy the latter; she had nothing but contempt for the rich, especially those pure-blood aphrodites who'd cast her out. Until Curt met Ashi, racism had been only an abstraction, a stupid and outmoded concept that died sometime in the twenty-first century. From her, he learned that it still existed, and came to hate it as much as she did.

For five Venusian sols – almost a week by the Gregorian calendar – the two of them lived together, ate together, lurked through the labyrinthine tunnels of the maze together, and thieved together. The only thing they didn't do was sleep together, or at least not in the same bed. Ashi knew that Curt desired her, but while she sometimes allowed him to hold her in his arms and kiss her, she wouldn't surrender herself to him. As gently as she could, Ashi explained that she'd never had sex either, mainly because she'd decided that she wouldn't until she was sure that it would be with someone whom she was confident would stay…not just for the night, but always.

"I can do that," Curt, sitting on his makeshift bedroll on the other side of the closet Ashi called home, told her. "I **want** to do that."

Ashi rested on the cot, back against the wall, hands folded and legs crossed. She smiled at him in the way that made him feel as if his blood was running faster, his heart beating more insistently. "I know you do, and I know why, too. But –"

"But what?"

Ashi looked down at her hands. "You're not going to stay because you can't." She lost her smile. "They're still looking for you, and it's only a matter of time before they catch you…and probably me, too." Curt started to object, and she held up a hand. "In your heart of hearts, you know it's true. Your friend Otho is going to find you, sooner or later –"

"We're only staying a week. Our visas expire the day after tomorrow."

"It's easy to get them extended. And, when he finds you, you and me are through."

And, she was right.

XV

THAT NIGHT, HE ACCOMPANIED HER on a job that took them back to Karpovgrad, not far from where the Hotel Venera was located. They'd been avoiding that part of the colony ever since Curt ran away, and he was anxious about having to return, but it couldn't be helped.

Jewelry wasn't the only thing Ashi stole. She told Curt that she'd recently been hired to acquire a priceless twentieth century antique from the home of a wealthy aphrodite.

"Easy job." Sitting beside him on her cot, Ashi ran a forefinger across her pad. The holographic image of the *objet d'art* – a doll-like figurine of a muscular male wearing a red, white, and blue costume, carrying a matching shield with a red star in its center – was replaced by a tiny model of the target: a Spanish-style hacienda, two stories tall, with a tile roof, surrounded by a high stucco wall. "Here's how we get in."

She pointed to the southeast corner of the house, where French windows led out onto a surrounding terrace. "The figure is in a display case in the study, which is on the first floor. Key locks on the doors. No security to speak of other than a couple of drones, and I can disable those with my jammer on the way in. The hard part is the wall. It's a little high, but once I'm over it, the rest should be easy."

"'Once **I'm** over it'?" Curt gave her a sidelong look. "Don't you mean, 'Once **we're** over it'?"

"No." Ashi shook her head. "It's not going to take both of us to get the thing. Once I've jammed the drones, it'll be better if just one of us goes in…less noise inside the house that way, and I don't want to wake up anyone upstairs. And if we **did** wake someone up and they heard two people downstairs, they'd probably call the proctors instead of trying to handle it themselves. And that's why I want you outside."

She pointed to the southern side of the wall surrounding the house. "You're going to be here, which is where I'm going over. You'll be my eyes and ears. If you spot anything that makes you think the law is on the way, you'll tell me and I'll drop everything and get out…this way, if I have to."

Her finger traveled through the miniature barred gate at the western side of the wall. Studying the holo, Curt contemplated everything Ashi had just told him. As she said, it seemed like a perfect plan, simple and uncomplicated. Still …

"I'm not sure why," he murmured, "but I don't like it."

"How come?"

"I don't know. It just seems…y'know…too easy."

"Oh, listen to the master thief!" She was smiling, but there was a hint of irritation in her eyes. "A week ago, you wouldn't have shoplifted a piece of candy. Now you're telling me how to –"

"I'm not trying to tell you how to do anything. I know you're an expert. It's just …"

Unable to complete his thought, he became silent. Ashi gave him a second to finish; when he didn't, she reached over and took his hand. "It's going to be fine. Really. I've done dozens of jobs like this, never been caught once. You're making it easier being outside because now I won't have to pay attention to anything except getting the item. That's why I want you to stay out of the house."

Curt still didn't like it, but Ashi wasn't giving him a choice. She'd made it clear to him that, as much as she liked having him around, she was the boss when it came to criminal activity…and almost everything they did was criminal. Part of being in love with her was that he was helpless against her will. Perhaps he wouldn't walk through an airlock if she'd asked him to, but everything just short of spacing himself was a viable request. If Ashi told him that she wanted to go to Earth and steal the Mona Lisa from the Louvre, he would've happily helped her, and to hell with everything Simon and Otho had tried to instill in him about right and wrong.

In the quiet hours of the night when the colony was dark and still, they emerged from a manhole just a hundred feet from the estate. A street lamp cast their shadows across the cobblestones as they hurried from the alley in which they'd emerged to a small park across from the house. Beneath the protective branches of an elm, they paused to study the premises.

The house was dark, its only light the wan glow of a carriage lamp beside the front door, which they could see through the iron filigree of the front gate. Nothing moved.

From a pocket within her cape, Ashi produced a coiled climbing rope. As she unfolded the tines of the attached grappling hook, Curt again admired her efficiency. She didn't wear night goggles – what little starlight penetrated the colony's windows didn't provide enough ultraviolet radiation for them to work effectively – but it was as if she could see in the dark. He'd learned many of the same tricks himself, during the long hours of training with Otho and Grag, but she made them look effortless.

A final wary glance up and down the street, a nervous tug at the shoulder strap of the black cotton rucksack on her back, then she gave him a nod. Together, they darted from behind the tree. Even their footsteps were silent as they sprinted toward the house, avoiding the pool of light cast by another street lamp. Within moments, they gained the shadows of the wall.

Ashi paused again to check the surroundings, then she stepped out onto the sidewalk, turned about, and twirled the hook and rope a couple of times before hurling it up and over the top of the wall. She'd evidently done this quite a bit, for the hook caught on the first try. Ashi yanked the rope to make sure it was secure, then her gloved hands found the knots at the bottom of the line.

Then, unexpectedly, she turned to Curt. Before he knew what she was doing, Ashi gently placed a hand around the back of his neck and pulled him close. Her cape's raised hood hid her face, but he could still see her eyes, their dark pupils dimly reflecting the streetlights.

"I know you love me," she whispered.

"Yes…yes, I do." He somehow managed to find his voice.

"Then I love you, too."

She kissed him, and again it felt for a moment as if everything else in the universe had vanished. Then, she let him go. An instant later, she'd grasped the rope again and was climbing, feet planted against the wall, sack dangling from her back.

Curt watched as she made her ascent, wondering why she'd done what she just had. Was it for luck? Or did she just think now was as good a time as any? He knew he was supposed to be on lookout, but he couldn't take his eyes off her, and didn't look away until she made it to the top of the wall.

Crouching low, Ashi took another moment to pull the rope up behind her. Curt watched as she glanced about the premises while gathering the line and tucking it, along with the grapple, into her cape. Confident that she was not being observed, she twisted about on her toes, grasped the top of the wall with her hands, and carefully swung herself over the other side. And then, she was gone.

Curt had an urge to trot over to the gate and see if he could spot her, but his task was to remain at this spot. If he had any reason to believe that the law had become alert to their presence, he was to break silence and contact her via Anni, using the local node they'd avoided until now. Likewise, if a prefect noticed him loitering here and was coming over to investigate, he was to calmly walk away; if questioned, he'd say that he was just out for a nocturnal stroll. Otherwise, he wasn't to move from this place until she came over the fence again.

Despite his anxiety, Curt found himself smiling. Tonight. Tonight, once the heist was done and they'd safely returned to her room. Tonight, they would …

"Curt."

At the sound of his name quietly being spoken from somewhere behind him, Curt whirled about. In the second that he hadn't been looking in that direction, a figure had stepped out from behind the corner of the wall past the gate. Curt couldn't see his face, but the voice was unmistakable.

Otho confirmed that it was him by stepping into the light.

"Curt, what are you doing?" Perhaps he'd sensed Curt's impulse to bolt and run, because he stopped where he was. "This is no place for you. You shouldn't be here."

"How did you –?"

Above him, another familiar sound: the soft whir of impellers. Curt looked up to see the Brain descending from above, his eyestalks weaving back and forth.

"He's right, lad," Simon Wright said. "How we found you isn't important just now. What matters is that the prefects have been alerted and they're on their way. If they find you here –"

"You'll be arrested," Otho finished. He was closer now. "We can't help you if that happens. C'mon, kid, let's get out of –"

"Don't call me that!" Curt was no longer bothering to keep his voice down. And even as he snapped at Otho, he opened his neural-net link to Ashi.

–Ashi, get out of there! The law is coming!

No answer, not even a subaudible click of acknowledgement.

Otho was almost close enough to touch him. He extended a hand. "Curt, let's go…!"

–Ashi, they've found me! Get out of there now! Curt stared up at the wall, helplessly searching for the girl. Still no answer.

"You can't help her, Curtis." Simon was nearly beside him now, at his level and coming closer, his manipulators extended. "Ashi Lenyr is already gone, and you –"

"How do you know her name?"

There was something in Simon's left claw. It flashed, and Curt fell into a darkness that didn't possess the sweet mystery he'd come to expect from the night.

XVI

Now...

"On final approach, Curtis," the Brain said.

Coming back to the present, Curt nodded. Through the porthole was impenetrable darkness – the recon pod still traveled in a bubble of invisibility – but the fantome field didn't affect the winds currents surrounding the tiny craft. A minute ago, there had been a short but violent episode of chop as the pod passed through a thermocline between atmospheric layers. Although he couldn't see anything, he knew that it meant the pod was closing in on the rendezvous point.

A computer screen on the panel above the porthole displayed an artificial image of the slowly descending skyhook. At the end of the tether, Scoopy's receiving port resembled an enormous silver pumpkin seed, its ellipsoid shape reducing atmospheric friction as it gradually came down. Along the underside, a large hatch yawned wide open, robotic grasping claws lowering from within. Although there wasn't a cargo dirigible to take aboard, Scoopy automatically put in operation the retrieval procedures whenever the tether descended.

On the other side of the receiving port, a thick cable of unbreakable graphene derived from Venusian regolith rose up into the sky. The tether was anchored within the port's central well by horizontal cables and crosspieces that gave it a degree of flexibility, while cylindrical elevator cars, some as large as the *Comet*, traveled up and down the tether, carrying raw ore up to Stratos. Along the outer edge of the port were recessed docking hatches, built to accommodate service vehicles.

"Three hundred feet and closing," Simon said. "There's a docking collar on the forward side, not far from the cargo hatch. I think I can get there."

"Can you get a hard seal?"

A pause. "Can't tell for certain, lad. Our hatch might not firmly fit the docking collar."

"How many minutes to contact?"

"Two minutes, thirty-two seconds."

"And how long is our window?"

"Approximately ninety seconds. No more than two minutes."

Curt frowned. They'd never thought this would be easy, but now it appeared this was going to be harder than expected. "Okay, it looks like I may have to jump for it. Depressurize the pod and get ready to pop the hatch."

"Are you sure you want to take the chance?" There was concern in Simon's electronic voice.

"Doesn't look like I have much choice, do I?" Curt had already loosened his shoulder straps. He reached beneath his seat for his lifepack harness and helmet. He fit the harness over his upper torso, making sure that its chest plate didn't cover the disk of the portable fantome generator mounted on the front of his skinsuit. The invisibility device was connected to its own battery pack on his belt. A short time ago, he and Simon had devised a partial solution to the problem of the fantome's intense energy drain; although he could keep the field active for only fifteen minutes, at least he no longer had to divert power from his plasma energy pistol if he needed to use both at once. He tightened the straps, then picked up the helmet and carefully lowered it over his head, clamping it firmly into place within the neck ring. A faint hiss told him that air was coming in through the rebreather unit on his back.

As he did all this, Curt's mind focused on the problem before him. The tether was coming down fast; if Simon's piloting wasn't in error, in just another minute or so the recon pod would be directly beneath the Skyhook when it reached to the furthest point of its cyclical descent. For a very short period — about a minute and a half, but no more than two — it would seem as if Scoopy was in a stationary position before beginning its long, slow ascent to orbit.

Time enough for a dirigible to be retrieved and pulled aboard. But time enough for the pod to hard-dock with the receiving port, get Curt aboard, then cut loose and move away before the tether began its ascent? Not bloody likely. If the pod couldn't safely dock with the skyhook in those few short seconds, Curt had just one chance to get aboard…

"Simon? Read me?" he said, testing the comlink.

"Loud and clear." The Brain's voice came through his headset.

"Shut down the fantome and pop the hatch."

"Wilco."

The porthole cleared. Suddenly, he could see outside: clouds far below, blue sky above. Then, seemingly coming out of nowhere, an immense curved surface descended before him. At its center was a small, open hatch, a narrow airlock revealed within.

"Docking with Stratos in fifteen seconds…fourteen…"

"Never mind the countdown." Standing up from his seat, Curt crouched low and grasped the rungs on either side of the porthole. Simon had already unsealed the hatch; Curt shoved it upward, and a savage wind snatched at him and threatened to yank him out of the tiny craft. He gritted his teeth as he grabbed hold of the hatch combing and braced himself. The airlock was only a few feet away, but the gap was unforgiving of a mistake; jump and miss, and there would be nothing to stop a long, lethal fall into the Venusian atmosphere below.

"Coming up fast. Three, two, one…now, Curt!"

Curt jumped.

A second of terror, and he was across the gap and inside the airlock.

"You're in," the Brain said. As if Curt didn't know.

Curt let out his breath, turned to look back. The pod was still there, but Simon was already closing the porthole hatch. As he watched, the pod began to fall away; the precious few seconds had passed, and now the skyhook was beginning its ascent.

"You're going to follow me up?" he asked

"Affirmative, but only for a little while. I can match speed with the tether and remain on station, but it'll get ahead of me before we breach the atmosphere."

Curt nodded. He was on his own, as he'd expected. "Any indication we've been spotted?"

A few seconds went by while the Brain tapped the colony's Anni node. "Negative. No one has a clue we're here."

"Good." At least there was that. By then, Curt had located the airlock control panel and flipped the proper switches. The outer hatch irised shut, and a pressure indicator above the inner hatch began to run from red to orange to green.

"I've reached the *Comet*. We're on channel F."

"Thanks." Until then, he and his crew back aboard the ship had been observing comlink silence. He touched the control pad on his left wrist, patching into the scrambled frequency the Futuremen used for long-distance communications. "*Comet*, this is Captain Future. Where are you now?"

Otho's voice came through. "On final approach to Venera Stratos. Trafco has cleared us for rendezvous and docking, but we've been waiting to hear from you. How's it going, chief?"

"I'm aboard, but Brain isn't. We couldn't dock the pod, so I jumped over and he's flying alongside Scoopy while he can."

"Mission is still go?"

"Affirmative. Go ahead and bring in the *Comet*."

"Wilco, but what are we going to tell whoever's going to be waiting for us when they don't see you?"

"I don't know," Curt said, a trifle impatiently. "Tell 'em I've got a cold –"

"Yeah, that's convincing."

"– or whatever. Look, I've got other things to worry about. Captain Future out."

He muted the comlink but didn't sign off, in case the *Comet* needed to get in touch with him or vice-versa. The pressure indicator had just flashed green; Curt undogged the inner airlock hatch and pushed it open.

The corridor that lay on the other side was narrow but well lit, its white metal walls lined with pressure doors. A low hum pervaded. There was no one in sight. From his earlier study of the receiving port's interior, Curt knew that this corridor ran inward to the central core. If the tether cable was indeed Starry Messenger's target, that's where he'd find them. The corridor was pressurized, but he kept his helmet on, visor lowered. He'd be needing suit air as soon he found the airlock at the other end of the corridor and entered the core.

"Okay, Simon, I'm heading for the core."

"Affirmative. Sorry I'm not there to help you."

Curt quietly snorted. "Don't worry, Brain. I think I can handle this by myself."

Simon's response was a rude, discordant buzz, his equivalent of a raspberry. Some time ago, the Futuremen had traced a lifewater ring to Ceres, where they'd discovered the source for the illegal drug that reversed aging but turned its users into addicts who died quickly if their supply was cut off. During the confrontation, one of the criminals they'd cornered had dropped his particle beam pistol. Because Curt and the others were outnumbered, Simon had snatched up the pistol and, holding it with both claws, aimed and fired on the closest thug.

In the heat of the moment, Simon forgot about the asteroid's low gravity. A person standing on the floor could easily handle the recoil, but not an airborne cyborg. The particle-beam took off the top of the other guy's head, but it also sent the Brain crashing against the stone wall behind him, breaking one of his eyestalks. Altogether, a humiliating experience. Shortly afterwards, Simon's mobility system was upgraded to make him more stable in midair, but no one had let him forget this incident. It was rare to see the Brain humbled.

"Fine," Simon groused. "Go ahead, save the day. Good luck."

Curt pulled the plasma-beam pistol – the plasmar, his unique weapon – from its holster. A brief whine as he pushed the button above the grip to charge the gun, then he headed down the corridor.

The core lay ahead.

XVII

THE SABOTEURS WERE EASY TO FIND.

There were three of them, two men and a woman, each wearing skinsuits, their helmet visors polarized opaque. The darkened helmets were the giveaway; the moment Curt saw this, he knew at once that they couldn't be laborers. There was no direct sunlight within the core, so they had no reason to darken their helmets. Not that they were making much of an attempt to hide what they were doing. Almost as soon as he cycled through the airlock leading to the core, he spotted the trio.

The receiving port's central core was a hollow shaft about eighty feet in diameter and sixty feet deep, the tether at its center resembling an enormous beanstalk. A network of jointed steel arms connected the tether to the core's inner walls; service catwalks ran along the shaft walls and across the top of the arms. The shaft was hollow all the way down; past the bottom of the tether cable, he could see distant cloud tops swirling beneath the open bay where cargo dirigibles were taken aboard and unloaded.

The saboteurs were atop an arm catwalk, about twenty feet to the left of the airlock Curt used to enter the core. While the woman stood guard, a particle beam rifle clasped in her arms, her two companions crouched beside the tether. It appeared that they were using an arc welder to solder something in place.

A bomb. Dynatomite, if he guessed correctly: TNT infused with uranium-235, a low-yield "dirty nuke" commonly used for asteroid mining. It wouldn't take much to sever the cable; its carbon nanofibers were tough, but a sufficiently strong blast would shred them like a birthday ribbon.

He hadn't been spotted, so Curt stayed within the airlock alcove. He switched his comlink to Anni mode, just on the off-chance that his helmet might not muffle his voice enough not to be heard by the people on the catwalk.

—Simon, this is Curt. You still there?

—I'm here, lad. What's going on?

—Found the bad guys. They're in the core, all right. Three of them. Looks like they're attaching an explosive device to the tether.

—How many? Just one?

Curt peeked out from the alcove. *—I see just the one they're working on.*

—Don't count on there being only one. They'd need more than that to sever the tether, and they may have set the others already.

— Understood. Call in an IPF strike team to…wait a sec.

The small gas-flame of the arc welder had ceased flickering. As Curt watched, the two men crouching beside the tether attached a smaller object to the bomb: a wireless detonator, Curt guessed. This was quickly done, then they picked up the torch and its fuel rig, stood up, and began backing away.

—They've finished arming the bomb, Curt said. *— If that's the last one, then IPF won't get here in time before they blow it. I've got to take 'em down.*

— Affirmative. Go get 'em, Captain Future.

Curt almost laughed. There was a time when he would've growled at anyone who called him by his childhood nickname. But President Carthew had insisted on adopting it as his IPF code name, and over the past few years, Curt had become accustomed to it. Strange as may be, it seemed as if the public **wanted** there to be someone called Captain Future. The president was right. People needed a hero …and like it or not, he'd been given the job.

Ashi would've loved that, he thought, and immediately shook his head. Why was he thinking of her just now? She was long in the past, and stuff like that only distracted him.

"Okay, then…here we go." Curt switched the plasmar to its stun setting, counted to three, then stepped out of the alcove and, clasping the gun with both hands, raised his weapon in the direction of the tether catwalk.

The woman standing guard spotted him immediately. She must have yelled something over the channel she was sharing with her companions, because they reacted by turning around to stare in the direction she was pointing, straight at Curt.

Before any of them could react, Curt fired. Not at the saboteurs, though, but at a more important target: the bomb. Before anything else, he needed to nullify the threat it posed. No way to reach the bomb and attempt to disarm it before someone triggered the detonator, so there was just one way to take care of it. He took careful aim and held his breath, then hoped for the best and squeezed the trigger.

The plasma beam, visible in the thin carbon-dioxide atmosphere as an expanding series of translucent rings, struck the device with enough force to shake apart the detonator without triggering it, rendering the dynatomite charge useless.

It took only a second, yet that was just long enough for the woman on the catwalk to return fire. She shot from the hip, though, and didn't give herself time

to draw a good bead. The crimson beam missed Curt and burned a thumb-sized hole in the metal wall a couple of feet to his left. By then, he was already in motion, lunging from the airlock to run down the circular walkway toward the catwalk entrance.

"Anni, patch me to wideband comlink!" he snapped. A single beep told him that Anni had complied. Crouching behind a railing support, he changed the plasmar's setting to Stun and aimed at the woman.

"This is Captain Future!" he yelled. "Throw down your weapons and surrender!"

He'd long since gotten over being self-conscious about his *nom de guerre.* Over the last few years, it had become known throughout the system, and while it may have once prompted smirks and giggles, now it prompted fear and respect. Many troublemakers now opted to drop their guns and put up their hands rather than face him or the Futuremen in a firefight that they'd probably lose. But not always. More often than not, his name earned a violent response.

The woman fired again, but if anything, her aim was even worse. The second shot went wide and burned a hole through the walkway. Curt leveled his gun at her, but before he could drop her, the two men with her drew their PB pistols and opened fire.

Their aim was better. One shot burned through the railing above Curt's head; any closer and it might have drilled the top of his helmet. Curt didn't linger behind the rail any longer. Leaping to his feet, he returned fire. The cascading rings of his plasma beam struck the closer of the two men square in the chest; dropping his PBP, he collapsed unconscious upon the catwalk.

His companion was less fortunate. He managed to get off one more shot before Curt winged him. It wasn't a direct hit, but he was leaning against the catwalk railing, so instead of falling backward, he toppled over the railing. Screaming, he plummeted down the shaft, disappearing through the open bottom of the central core. If he was lucky, he'd lose consciousness before he entered the acidic clouds far below; not even his skeleton would reach the ground.

Curt was sorry that happened, but he didn't have time to pity the man. The woman had disappeared. Sometime in the last few seconds, she'd turned to run back the way she'd come, toward the tether. Curt looked for her, but didn't spot her. She must be on the other side of the thick cable, using it as a shield.

Curt ran a few steps down the circular walkway surrounding the tether. Sure enough, there she was, hurrying down another catwalk, heading for the opposite side of the shaft.

He realized what she was doing. Elevators for both passengers and freight ran alongside the tether cable. One of the passenger elevators was at the end of the catwalk the saboteurs had used to get to the cable, its lozenge-shaped car already waiting. The logical destination would be the colony far above; if she could reach Venera Stratos itself, she could lose her pursuer.

She was too far to reach…but not to shoot.

Curt stopped midway down the catwalk. There was nothing between him and the woman except distance. The gun came up again, this time in both hands. The interesting thing about the plasma-beam pistol was that he didn't have to be too accurate with it; since the beam spread out after firing, so long as he was within range of his target, sharpshooting was unnecessary.

He drew a bead on the woman, who by now had reached the other side of the shaft and was running along its walkway. He didn't fire at once, though, but instead tracked her as she raced to the elevator. She hadn't looked around to see what he was doing; obviously, she thought Curt was still hot on her heels.

She reached the elevator and slapped the palm of her hand against its oversized call button. As its doors slid open, Curt fired. Concentric rings of energy rippled across the shaft; they hit the woman in the center of her back, and even her life-support pack wasn't enough to shield her; she was slammed face forward into the elevator. She was unconscious before she touched the floor. Fortunately, she didn't fall all the way in; from the hips down, her body lay outside the car, blocking the doors and preventing them from closing again.

Curt smiled, silently congratulating himself. He hadn't shot her while she was running along the walkway because he'd been afraid that she'd topple over the railing and follow her companion to a horrible death. He'd learned to have an aversion to killing his foes, even when he was still able to do so unless it was unavoidable. In this case, it was unnecessary to kill this woman, and his conscience was clear about shooting a fleeing suspect in the back.

As he trotted down the catwalk, he reactivated his comlink. "Brain, *Comet*, it's Curt…Captain Future." Almost forgot himself there. "Third suspect down. Moving in to apprehend. Immediate threat nullified, but I still want that IPF backup."

"They're on the way, chief," Otho said.

"Good work, lad," the Brain added. "Well done."

Reaching the tether, he found the place where the terrorists had been working on the bomb. A quick glance to make sure it was a broken mess, then he continued down the catwalk. The woman hadn't yet moved; he had no doubt that she was out cold, but he wanted to reach her before the stun wore off.

She was still face down, half-in and half-out of the elevator, when he got to her. She'd dropped the rifle; Curt took a second to use his foot to push it out of her reach. He kept the plasmar trained on her back. She could be faking it; he'd had that happen before, and had learned to be ready for it.

But she wasn't shamming. She didn't respond when Curt ordered her to get up, and there was no reaction when he prodded her side with his boot. She was unconscious all right, and would probably stay that way for some time.

"Suspect apprehended," he said. "Otho, dock at the hub –"

"Docking now, chief," Otho said.

"Great. Soon as you're in, send Grag down to help me bring her in."

"Wilco." This time, it was Grag's monotone voice who spoke to him. "I'm on the way."

Curt knew that it would take a while for Grag to reach him. And before the robot got there, there was something he had to do.

He switched the gun to his left hand, squatted down on one knee, and reached down to push the unconscious woman over on her side. Once he could see the curved face plate of her helmet visor, he reached forward to her slack left wrist, found the suit controls, and depolarized the helmet.

He couldn't have said exactly when it had been during the last few minutes, or even why, that he'd begun to suspect who she might be. Maybe the way she moved somehow seemed familiar, triggering subconscious recognition. Perhaps it may have simply been because this was Venera Stratos and once, long ago, he'd met a girl here. Even so, as her helmet visor cleared, Curt found himself hoping, even praying, that his hunch was wrong and that he wouldn't recognize the face he'd see.

To his horror, he did.

XVIII

G‌RAG WAS IN THE *COMET'S* PASSENGER compartment when Curt came down the ladder from the flight deck. The robot squatted on his hips on one side of the mid-deck, a small rubber ball in his metal hand. Two small creatures, a brown and white moonpup and something that looked like an enormous larva, sat at his feet; the moonpup was giving Grag his undivided attention, but it was hard to tell what the eyeless, mouthless, limbless thing next to him was thinking.

As Curt stepped off the ladder, Grag tossed the ball toward the other side of the mid-deck. Now that the *Comet* had departed from Venera Stratos and was on its way back to the Moon, the warp bubble had been activated, bringing artificial gravity to the craft's interior. The ball bounced off the far wall; the agile little dog was already there, ready to hop up on his hind legs and snatch it from the air.

"Ooooog!" moaned the larva-like thing at Grag's feet.

Curt looked down at Oog. The creature – Simon believed it to be an anamorphic pseudo-life form from the Deneb system, left behind on Mars by alien visitors countless centuries ago – had begun to generate stubby legs; one end was forming a neck and head, the other a long, slender tail. And because it was no longer pale white, but instead blotched tan and brown, it appeared that it was making an effort to transform into a facsimile of the moonpup.

"I thought Oog could make himself resemble Eek," Curt said. The moonpup pranced before him, showing off the ball in his mouth.

"He can." Grag's smooth face, featureless save for a pair of wide round eyes, turned toward him. "It just takes a little while, that's all." He held out an open hand, gesturing for Eek to bring the ball back. "That's why we're playing ball…to improve his anamorphic reflexes, get him used to changing faster. And give Eek a little exercise, too."

A dry smile that Curt didn't much feel like making. "And here I thought you were doing this because it was fun." He glanced at the door behind Grag. "Have you heard from her yet?"

"No, she's been quiet. But, –" his ovoid head cocked slightly as if listening carefully, an oddly human gesture for a robot with no visible ears "–she's awake. Her respiration, cardiac rate, and skin temperature indicate consciousness."

Grag was tapped into one of the guest room's biosensors; funny that he'd try to make it sound like he was actually listening at the door. Curt was not in the mood to contemplate again the robot's continuing efforts to emulate human behavior, though. "Okay, I'm going in," he said, and Grag obediently rose and stepped aside for him.

The *Comet* had six small passenger cabins on its mid-deck. Three were for Curt, Otho, and their IPF liaison, Lt. Joan Randall, when she traveled with them on a mission. The other three, although usually occupied by invited guests, were also designed to serve as holding cells for prisoners. Curt slid open a panel beside cabin four and tapped a code number into a keypad.

A soft click came from the door as it unlocked. Curt reached for the handle, then hesitated. If she'd just awakened, then she probably didn't know where she was. When the guest cabin was in cell mode, the porthole was polarized opaque and data access was blocked. Here inside the *Comet*'s warp bubble, it was even possible to mistake the presence of gravity for meaning that they were still on Venera Stratos.

He could make this simple and just leave her alone. Keep her isolated in her quarters until the *Comet* reached the Moon, where she'd be transferred to an IPS pinnace and put in the custody of the SolCol justice system. So she didn't have to know where she was, or who was taking her to justice. As Captain Future, his involvement with this whole incident could end there. Perhaps it **should** end there. But...

But he opened the door and went in anyway.

The cabin was dark, though not completely. In the wan light coming in through the door, Curt could see the woman curled up on the fold-down bunk. Her slim figure was hidden beneath the heavy quilt; her hair formed a dark halo around her head. Her eyes were closed, and it appeared that she was asleep.

A sleeping beauty, or so she'd have him believe. He wondered if she knew how many times he'd watched her sleep.

Gazing at her from the doorway, Curt reflected upon how much Ashi Lanyr had matured in the ten years since he'd last seen her. A decade was a long time, of course, so of course he wouldn't immediately recognize her, but even so...he shook his head. No. He remembered her as a teenage girl; this was an adult woman.

An adult woman whom he had just arrested on suspicion of terrorism. Ashi had been a thief, and he'd learned long ago, the hard way, that she could not be trusted. Nonetheless, he could scarcely believe that she'd join an outfit like Starry Messenger or attempt to bring destruction to her own home. What had happened? How could she ...?

"Hello, Curt," she said quietly.

Her voice, muffled by the blanket, was a murmur, but it could just as well have been a scream. There it was: she knew who he was. Few people in the system knew Captain Future's real name, but she was one of them. No sense in trying to pretend otherwise.

"Hello, Ashi," he said. "You awake? Ready for the light?"

"Yeah…yeah, sure. Lights on."

She rolled over and sat up as the ceiling panels glowed to life. She still wore the light blue bodysuit she'd had on beneath her space gear. Otho had undressed her in the cabin after she was brought aboard, and Curt had stayed out of the room. He was doing his best not to stare, but he couldn't help but notice: Ashi had grown up, indeed, in all the best ways…

Well, in the ways that showed, anyway.

"I guess…" Curt stopped, coughed nervously through a dry throat. "I mean, I guess I'm surprised you recognized me. I didn't know it was you until…" His voice trailed off.

"Until you shot me from behind?" She shrugged. "Well, I suppose you did what you thought you had to do. And sure, I knew it was you." A tight smile. "If you don't want people to recognize your face, Captain Future, maybe you ought to wear a mask."

"Don't want to come off like a twencen superhero, that's why." Curt stepped the rest of the way into the room, closing the door behind him. "Sorry I had to take you down that way. I couldn't let you escape."

"Yes, well…it wouldn't have been the first time, would it?"

Curt said nothing. He studied her, trying to divine the implication of what she'd said. "If you think you're telling me something I don't already know, you're wrong," he said at last. "The last time I saw you, that night…it was you who tipped off Simon and Otho where we'd be." It wasn't a question or a guess, but something he'd known for a long time.

Her eyelids flickered. "They told you?" she asked, and he nodded. "How long did it take them?"

"A few days. Not until after we got home. Simon knew my heart had been broken, and although he was tempted to let me go on believing that he and Otho had somehow tracked me down, in the end he decided that it was best that I know the truth…you'd sent a message to our hotel suite, informing them that I was with you, that I was safe but that I needed to be picked up, and exactly where and when I'd be. They were there, hiding in the shadows, waiting and watching, and as soon you disappeared and as I was alone, they moved in."

"And that's it, huh? You know everything."

"No, that's not it, and I don't know everything." Curt let out his breath, looked down, and shook his head. "I don't know why you did that. To this day, I don't know why you ..."

He couldn't bring himself to complete the thought. Ashi did it for him. "Betrayed you? Is that what you mean?" Still not looking at her, he nodded. "If that's the way you see it," she went on, her tone softening but little, "if that's going to be what you keep telling yourself, then anything I say won't matter." She paused. "But I didn't do it to betray you, Curt. I did it to save you."

His eyes came up, locking on hers. "What?"

Swinging her legs over the side of the bed, Ashi folded her hands in her lap and regarded him with dark and solemn eyes. Eerily, she looked very much like the way she did that first night they were together, in her hideaway beneath the habitat floor. "When I first found you, when I lured you from your room and got you to run away with me, I thought I'd found a kindred spirit...a kid a lot like myself, an outcast angry at the world. And perhaps you were, just a little bit...but after a few days, I knew I'd pegged you wrong. Maybe you were a misfit, even sort of a fugitive with the fake name and all, but you were no criminal." A smile touched the corners of her mouth. "You didn't have it in your heart to be a thief. And being a thief was what I was all about back then."

"**You** were what I had in my heart." Curt blurted it out before he could stop himself.

Her smile became melancholic, and it was her turn to look away. "I know...and I'd be lying if I said I didn't feel something for you, too. I loved the time we spent together, but the truth is, if I'd let it go on much longer, it would've ended badly. For both of us."

'You mean, you were afraid we'd get caught."

"Don't you think that was inevitable?" She looked at him again. "You were an amateur, I was a pro, and I didn't have time...or much inclination, really...to try to teach you things it had taken me years to learn. So yeah, we would've been busted, sooner or later. And believe me, it would've gone down just as hard for you as it would for me. Maybe even more, if they'd discovered that you weren't who you said you were."

Curt didn't say so, but her conjecture was valid, and even more than she suspected. If he'd been arrested by the aphrodite prefects, it was unlikely that his false identity as Rab Cain would've remained intact. And if it had been discovered that he was actually Curt Newton, a boy presumed to have perished along with his well-known parents some fifteen years earlier, it would have made the system newsnets...and Victor Corvo would have found out that he was still alive. That would've been the worst outcome of all, for Curt would've never

gained justice for the murder of his parents. Not before Corvo found a way to have him, Simon, and Otho liquidated in order to protect his secret.

"It had to be this way," Ashi was saying, and now her voice had become pleading. "Don't you see? I…I loved you, too, but there was no way we could –"

"All right. That's enough." Curt raised a hand. "I'm just sorry it had to be –"

He stopped himself before he could finish what he was about to say: *I'm just sorry it had to be me who took you down. I've always hoped I'd see you again, but not this way…not as Captain Future.*

Anything else that he might say to her, though, could only bring hurt to either or both of them. And, they'd hurt each other enough already. "Well…that's all I think I want to hear from you," he said, "and I'm not sure if you'd want to hear what I have to say, so maybe I better get to the cockpit. We'll be arriving at Luna in just a few minutes –"

"Just a few **minutes?**" She stared at him, incredulous. "Don't you mean –?"

"The *Comet* is a very fast ship. We'll be there soon." Curt turned to the door. "Grag is standing just outside. Ask him if you need anything." A brief smile. "He's a robot, but don't think to put anything past him…he's a lot smarter than most of his make and model type."

"So I've heard." Ashi settled back against her bunk, raising her long legs to hug her knees within her arms. It was a casual move, but Curt wondered if she had any idea how alluring she was just then. "You've become famous, you know. I've been following your exploits for quite a while."

He stopped at the door, turning his head to look over his shoulder at her. "And you say you recognized Captain Future as the kid who once ran away with you?"

Another coy smile. "How could I miss that red hair?" The smile faded. "And I had a feeling," she quietly added, "that if there was anyone who'd stop me from doing what my friends and I meant to do, it was going to be you."

"Are you sorry that it was?"

Once more, Ashi looked away. "Go on," she muttered, "get out of here."

There was nothing more to be said. He discovered that he didn't even want to know why she'd tried to sabotage the tether, except that she was probably right: she was a criminal, and maybe the steps from thief to terrorist weren't as many he might have once believed.

In any case, her life had gone in one direction, and his had gone in another. And it was too late to change that now.

Curt left the cabin, softly closing the door behind him. Grag was still outside, but he was no longer playing ball with Oog and Eek. The robot sat still, emotionless round eyes focused straight ahead. Curt didn't know if he'd overheard the conversation, or much care if he had.

He stood outside for a moment. Then he took a deep breath and headed for the ladder. The *Comet* would soon be entering Earth's cislunar traffic pattern; Captain Future was needed on deck.

XIX

Inside the guest cabin, Ashi Lanyr gazed out the porthole above her bunk. She turned off the ceiling panels as soon as Curt left. She'd always preferred the darkness; it spoke to her soul, which had been without light for so long that she'd accepted it as her natural condition. In the darkened cabin, she smiled to herself.

All was going to plan.

She was aboard the *Comet,* in the custody of Captain Future and the Futuremen. And while it had been difficult to see Curt again – she'd never forgotten him, although she'd never felt the same love for the boy that he once did for her – she was satisfied with the way everything had come out. It was unfortunate that one of her Starry Messenger comrades had lost his life, but everyone involved in the mission was aware of the risk of death and had accepted it. If the plan succeeded, and Ashi was confident that it would, then his sacrifice wouldn't be in vain.

So Ashi Lanyr relaxed. Soon, the *Comet* would be receiving a message that would cause Curt to change his plans. Soon, he and the Futuremen would be on their way elsewhere, to another mission at the far end of the solar system. And if all went well, soon they would enter the trap that had been set for them…a trap in which she was the bait that dear, lovely Curt had eagerly taken.

Soon, soon, very soon…

Captain Future Will Return

In

The Return Of Ul Quorn, Book II:

The Guns Of Pluto

IN THEIR NEXT ADVENTURE, Curt Newton, the Futuremen, and Joan Randall (no, she hasn't been forgotten!) race fast as light itself to Cold Hell, the Solar Coalition's maximum security prison on Pluto. An uprising among the prisoners is underway, instigated by the mysterious nemesis known as the Black Pirate. Yet nothing about this attempted breakout is what it seems, for the Pirate and his band have another plan in mind, one that will threaten the peace and safety of the entire solar system…and Captain Future is a factor in it! Surprises, suspense, and a familiar face or two await you when our heroes find themselves in the bullseye of…"The Guns of Pluto."

A Brief History Of Captain Future

(or, How I Resurrected an 80-Year-Old Space Hero & Gave Him a New Zap Gun)

NOW THAT *CAPTAIN FUTURE* has been relaunched, and I've undertaken the happy task of writing the first new Captain Future series since 1951, the obvious question is: why would anyone want to bring back an all-but-forgotten character from science fiction's pulp era?

The short answer is: because I can, and because it's fun.

The next obvious question is: who is Captain Future, and why does he matter?

That answer is rooted in the history of science fiction itself.

≈

IN 1939, BETTER PUBLICATIONS was one of the leading producers of pulp magazines, with a line-up that included two science fiction titles, *Thrilling Wonder Stori*es and *Startling Stories*. Yet, they didn't have a hero pulp, a magazine devoted to the adventures of a single character; some leading examples of the time were Street & Smith's *The Shadow* and *Doc Savage,* or Popular Publications' *The Spider* and *G-8 and His Battle Aces.* So, Better Publications publisher Leo Margulies and editor Mort Weisinger decided to launch one of their own.

Because their "scientifiction" magazines – they were still using this Gernsbeck-era neologism even though "science fiction" had lately become the preferred term – were selling well, they decided to go in that direction. They drafted a rough outline for a weird, macrocephalic scientist-hero called Mr. Future ("Wizard of Science"), then turned to one of their most reliable writers to flesh out the concept.

Edmond Hamilton was a popular author of early American science fiction; his most famous novel, *The Star Kings*, has seldom been out of print for very long since it was first published. Largely forgotten today, however, is the fact that he was one of the principal creators of the subgenre that later came to known as space opera. His novella "Crashing Suns," the first story of his Interplanetary

Patrol series, was published in the August 1928 issue of *Weird Tales*. In the very same month, though, two stories appeared in *Weird Tales'* competitor *Amazing Stories*: the first installment of *The Skylark of Space* by Edward E. Smith, and the novella "Armageddon 2419 A.D." by Philip Francis Nowlan. Smith's novel became one of the most influential SF stories of all time, while Nowlan's story formed the basis for the Buck Rogers comic strip and the multi-media franchise that followed, so those two authors got most of the credit for inventing space opera.

On the other hand, "Crashing Suns" was where many of the subgenre's elements – space battles, alien menaces, larger than life heroics – were introduced, and anyone who's ever written a story that uses these now-familiar tropes owes a debt to Ed Hamilton, whether they know it or not. Hamilton was a pioneer, but sadly, pioneers don't always get the recognition they deserve.

Nevertheless, during the pulp era of the 30's, he became famous among SF fans as "World Wrecker Hamilton," the author of swashbuckling space adventures like *Beyond the Universe* and *The Three Planeteers*. He was a mainstay of *Amazing* and also its competitors *Astounding, Thrilling Wonder*, and *Startling*. So, it made perfect sense for Margulies and Weisinger to hire him to write the adventures of Mr. Future and his companions.

But, Ed Hamilton was no hack. Not content to mindlessly bash out novels based on Leo and Mort's *précis*, he studied the outline for Mr. Future and determined which parts didn't make sense or limited the potential for an ongoing series, then tossed out the stuff that didn't work and created a character of his own. While traces of other pulp and comics heroes can clearly be seen – there's a strong Doc Savage influence, not to mention a noticeable similarity to Batman's origins – so very little remained of Mr. Future after Hamilton got through with him that it's safe to say that Captain Future was pretty much his creation.

Captain Future was publicly announced at the first World Science Fiction Convention, held in New York City over the Fourth of July weekend of 1939, and the Winter 1940 issue of *Captain Future, Wizard of Science* appeared several months later, with *Captain Future and the Space Emperor* (originally titled *The Horror on Jupiter)* as the first novel. While Curt Newton and the Futuremen were not the first SF pulp heroes – C. L. Moore's Northwest Smith, Harry Bates and Desmond Hall (aka Anthony Gilmore)'s Hawk Carse, and Neil R. Jones' Professor Jameson came first – they were the first to have their own magazine.

However, it was not an auspicious debut. John W. Campbell, Jr. had recently assumed the editorship of *Astounding* and, together with a stable of new writers like Robert A. Heinlein, Isaac Asimov, Theodore Sturgeon, and A. E. Van Vogt, had begun transforming SF into a mature form of literature. This era eventually came to be known as science fiction's "Golden Age," and compared to what was going on in *Astounding*, the old-school scientifiction published in *Captain Future* looked out of touch and juvenile.

Nor did it help that Hamilton had to write these novels fast, very fast. Despite the fact that *Captain Future* was a quarterly published just four times a year, Mort Weisinger – by some accounts not an editor beloved by most of the writers who worked for him – imposed absurdly short deadlines on Hamilton, demanding that he deliver the magazine's 40,000-word feature novels in just a couple of weeks. The late Julius Schwartz, Hamilton's friend and agent who'd later become the legendary editor-in-chief of DC Comics, once told me that he and Ed used to brainstorm Captain Future plots while riding the New York city bus down to Better Publications's offices on 48th Street. The Captain Future stories were fun, but most of them weren't among Hamilton's best work, and it showed.

Nonetheless, *Captain Future, Wizard of Science* (later retitled *Captain Future, Man of Tomorrow*) gained a following. Hamilton's stories weren't cutting-edge SF, but they were entertaining, and it was hard not to like Curt Newton and the Futuremen. The letters pages were lively, with many readers proclaiming the magazine to be their favorite. Robert Silverberg and Harlan Ellison read the magazine as kids, Ray Bradbury and Fredric Brown published early short stories in its back pages, and the great literary essayist S. J. Perelman enjoyed the premiere issue enough to write a tribute, "Captain Future, Block That Kick!" for *The New Yorker*.

"Beside Captain Future, Wizard of Science," Perelman wrote, "Flash Gordon and the Emperor Ming pale to a couple of nursery tots chewing on Holland rusk." Whatever that is.

Seventeen issues of *Captain Future* were published during the early 40s, with Hamilton writing all but two of the novels (those were produced by Joseph Samachson under the house name Brett Sterling, which Hamilton sometimes shared as well). The wartime paper shortage killed all but the most popular pulps, though; the final issue was cover-dated Spring 1944. That issue's feature novel, *Days of Creation*, was written by Samachson, but Hamilton had already turned in the next adventure, *Red Sun of Danger*. It was published in the Spring 1945 issue of *Startling Stories*, followed by *Outlaw World* in the Winter 1946 issue. The final Captain Future novel, *The Solar Invasion*, appeared in the Fall 1946 issue; it was written by Manly Wade Wellman, and didn't represent his best work either, which is unfortunate, for Wellman would go on to write the better-known John the Balladeer fantasy series.

Captain Future disappeared for a few years before being reintroduced in the January 1950 issue of *Startling*, in a new novelette by Edmond Hamilton appropriately titled "The Return of Captain Future." This was the first of a series of stories that sought to establish a more mature version of the character, now referred to as Curt Newton more often than Captain Future. Some pulp aficionados, myself included, suspect that they may have been secretly co-written with Hamilton's wife, the illustrious Leigh Brackett. Seven Captain Future stories were published in *Startling* over the course of the next couple of years, but in the May 1951 issue a sidebar accompanied "Birthplace of Creation," announcing that Curt Newton and the Futuremen were "taking an indefinite leave of absence."

"If their fortunes permit," the editorial stated, "they may, in time, be back in the pages of this magazine to render their incredible affairs. So, do not say good-bye but farewell."

And so, the curtains closed on Curt Newton and his crew. But, the curtains didn't remain shut forever.

In the late 60s, there was a resurgence of interest in the pulp heroes of the 30s and 40s. After Bantam Books had a surprise hit with their paperback republication of the Doc Savage adventures (and, less successfully, a short series of Shadow novels), other publishers jumped on the bandwagon. Ballentine and Ace reissued Edgar Rice Burroughs' Tarzan and John Carter of Mars novels, Berkley reprinted the Spider and G-8, Lancer reissued the Conan series, and porn publisher Corinth attempted to go mainstream by bringing back the Phantom Detective, Secret Agent X, Doctor Death, and Operator 5.

Not to be left out, Popular Library reprinted Captain Future. It was a mixed blessing, though. Although the covers of first three books featured lovely Frank Frazetta paintings and the fourth cover was by Jeffrey Jones, subsequent covers reprinted mediocre art from Germany's *Perry Rhodan* magazines. The novels weren't reprinted in order of publication; the first, *Danger Planet* by Brett Sterling, was actually *Red Sun of Danger*, the next-to-last novel of the original series, and the final Popular Library reprint to appear was *Captain Future and the Space Emperor,* the 1939 novel that introduced Captain Future in the first place. Several of the best adventures were skipped entirely. But, at least, they were out there, waiting for a new generation to discover them.

That's where I come in.

≈

WHEN I WAS ELEVEN YEARS OLD, just a couple of months before the Apollo 11 moon landing, I found one of those paperback reprints on a drugstore spinner rack. By then, I'd been reading SF for several years. Although I was still in elementary school, I was already reading way above my grade level; Heinlein juveniles alternated with Ace Science Fiction Specials and the monthly Science

Fiction Book Club main selections. But lately, I'd discovered Doc Savage, the Shadow, and Conan, and had fallen in love with the pulp heroes of the 30s.

When I found my first Captain Future, *Outlaws of the Moon,* I realized that it belonged to a kind of pulp SF not seen in decades. Yeah, it was old-fashioned and a bit dated, but who cared? It was a lot of fun. I read as many of the other reprints as I could find – *The Comet Kings, Planets in Peril,* and *Captain Future's Challenge* – and searched for more.

Yet, just as eleven is the perfect age to discover pulp fiction, sixteen is the perfect age to grow out of it. I got tired of these kind of stories about the same time I began to pay serious attention to girls. Along with the other pulp characters whose adventures I adored, Captain Future was left behind on the long, awkward road to adulthood. At some point, I forgot about him…

But, not entirely.

In the mid-90's, a few years after I launched my own career as a SF writer, I started thinking about pulp fiction again…specifically, how the space opera of yesteryear contrasted with the more serious SF of the postmodern era. This line of thought brought me back to Captain Future. I'd long since given away my Captain Future paperbacks. so I combed second-hand bookstores for the Popular Library reprints, re-reading them and taking notes as I did. Then, with permission from Edmond Hamilton's literary estate, I wrote a novella, "The Death of Captain Future."

That story is best described as a satirical homage, and when it was published in *Asimov's Science Fiction,* most readers understood where I was coming from, although a few purists objected to what I'd done. "The Death of Captain Future" received the Hugo and Seiun awards in 1996 and was short-listed for several other awards, including the Nebula. Since then, the story has been anthologized and translated many times. Despite the title, though, it's not really about Captain Future. Nor is its sequel, "The Outlaw of Evening Star," even though it was intended to be less satirical and more like traditional space opera. The second story was nowhere near as successful as the first, though, and that dissuaded me from writing a third story. Two Captain Future stories were enough; time to move on.

Over the next couple of decades, though, while I worked on other projects like the Coyote series or stand-alone novels like *V-S Day* and *Arkwright,* my mind kept returning to Captain Future…or rather, **my** version of Captain Future. I began to realize that, if I wanted to write this kind of pulp fiction, I ought to discard the satirical element and simply write straight-ahead space opera, old-school but yet revised and updated for the new age.

What I needed to do was write a new Captain Future novel.

≈

ANOTHER THING OCCURRED during this time: I became ill.

It began with a bad stomach ache one Saturday night at the local movie theater, gut pains so awful that I had my wife Linda rush me to the local hospital as soon as the movie was over. What we thought was ordinary food poisoning turned out to be something much more serious: acute pancreatitis, probably brought on by years of heavy drinking (man, did I love beer!). But even after I tapered off my beer and wine consumption and eventually quit drinking entirely, the attacks continued, each severe enough to land me in the hospital again. Eventually, I'd have my gall bladder and half of my pancreas removed in separate operations. But, for twelve years no one knew what was causing these episodes or how to stop them (we eventually did; a mutant gene in my personal genome preconditions me to chronic pancreatitis, and there's little I can do about it except not drink, smoke, or eat fatty food).

During one hospital stay, I found myself bored and wanting to do something besides just read or watch TV. As it so happened, one of the ebooks on my iPad was *Captain Future and the Space Emperor*. Re-reading this for the first time in decades, I began to perceive how Captain Future could be updated for a twenty-first century readership. Linda had already brought me a notebook and pens in case I wanted to write, so I took notes as I read, jotting down not only the important elements of Ed Hamilton's original creation – character names and descriptions, names of organizations, locations, technology, and so forth – but, also my thoughts on how to reinvent them.

The approach I took was to update Captain Future much the same way James Bond, Sherlock Holmes, the *Star Trek* series, and various Marvel and DC superheroes have been periodically revised. From the get-go, it was clear that just about everything in Hamilton's original novels would have to be reworked. In the six or seven decades that have elapsed since the first story in the series was published, our scientific knowledge and technology have made such vast advances that any attempt to write a Captain Future novel the same way Hamilton did during the 40s would have been immediately doomed to self-parody…and I didn't want to do "retro sci-fi."

Although Captain Future gradually became forgotten in the US – not a lot of American fans read the Popular Library paperbacks, and fewer still remembered them fondly – in the late 70's, he was rediscovered in Asia, Europe, and parts of the Arab world, thanks to the Japanese anime studio Toei. In the wake of the first big *Star Wars* craze, Toei produced an anime series, *Captain Future,* that was loosely adapted from the Hamilton novels. With a certain stylistic look that was *Star Wars*-influenced, the Captain Future anime was a hit in Japan, Germany,

France, Italy, and Saudi Arabia, where it was alternately known as *Capitaine Flam, Capitan Futuro,* and *Adventures of the Space Knights.* Tons of Captain Future merchandise – toys, comic books, trading cards, puzzles, bento boxes and chopsticks – were licensed; they're all scarce now and in demand, fetching hefty prices when they appear on eBay.

However, the one place where the series was not popular was in the country of Captain Future's birth. A badly translated and edited English-language version, with a theme song so dumb that it seemed to make sure that kids would switch channels, was syndicated in America, but unlike similar anime imports like *Star Blazers* and *Captain Harlock,* the series was little seen and even less appreciated. Indeed, following publication of my own Captain Future stories, the only fan response I've received that makes mention of the anime has come from European and Asian readers who, as kids, ran home every afternoon after school to catch their favorite show.

I knew about the Japanese anime and watched the few English-language episodes that were released on VHS tapes in 80's, but made a conscious decision not to emulate it. That version of Captain Future was meant for kids, while I was writing for a young-adult-and-older audience. So, fans of the anime Captain Future shouldn't expect to see the show being reprised here (well, okay, I imported one thing I like: the *Comet's* one-man jitney, the Cosmoliner, which I've adapted as the *Comet II*'s recon pod).

Although I was updating Hamilton's characters and concepts for *Avengers of the Moon*, at the same time, I sought to retain the spirit of the original. Early on, I made the conscious decision to avoid the sort of grim, dark future that has been prevalent in science fiction through the last couple of decades. The Solar Age of the new Captain Future timeline, the late twenty-third and early twenty-fourth centuries, would be a new Renaissance in which humankind has spread out across the solar system while simultaneously splitting into several different offshoots – collectively known as *Homo cosmos* – genetically adapted for survival on different worlds. And, while these aresians, aphrodites, kronians, and kuiperians would be different from the Martians, Venusians, Saturnians, and Plutonians of the original Hamilton stories, their role would be much the same: they would be denizens of our solar system's worlds, similar to humankind, but also extraterrestrial if not wholly alien, their relationship to *Homo sapiens* both friendly and not-so-friendly.

Likewise, the technology was also updated. Gone are the "rocket tubes" of Captain Future's ship, the *Comet*; I used nuclear ion-plasma engines for the updated version in *Avengers of the Moon*, which was originally a racing yacht belonging to Roger Newton, Curt's father. In "Captain Future in Love," where the *Comet II* is introduced, I incorporated a warp drive into the *Comet's* larger and more powerful descendant. An artist friend, Rob Caswell, helped me refurbish both vessels; his design for the *Comet II* appears in this volume.

For the first *Comet*, Rob and I retained the general teardrop shape of the original, but otherwise put it through stem-to-stern revisions. The invisibility device that Curt uses to elude his foes was likewise retained, but I renamed it the fantome (French for phantom) generator and extrapolated it in terms of stealth technology. Interestingly, I didn't have to do many changes here; Hamilton wasn't far off the mark when he described how something like this might theoretically work (and invisibility itself is no longer as hypothetical as it once was). For the second version, the *Comet II* that makes its debut in this book, Rob and I decided to break from tradition and design a completely new ship for Captain Future that, among other things, would utilize the FTL warp-drive theorized by the Mexican physicist Miguel Alcubierre. Working from my specifications and suggestions, Rob designed a ship that Ed Hamilton probably couldn't have imagined in the late 30's, largely because the *Comet II* utilizes technology that hadn't been conjectured in Hamilton's time. The streamlined lander and its detachable warp torus is a radical departure, yes, but so was the *Comet* of the Japanese anime, a handsome but utterly implausible craft.

Another revision is Captain Future's gun. In the original novels, it was little more than a garden-variety ray gun, and I wanted something more interesting than that. The cover art by Wesso on the original magazines often showed Captain Future firing what looks like translucent smoke rings. Taking this as a jumping-off point, I approached my colleagues in Sigma, an informal group of SF writers who often act as national security consultants, for suggestions. They came up with the "plasmar" – a gun that fires toroid-shaped charges of electrical plasma energy. The gun can be set to either stun or kill, and the shots appear (in an atmospheric environment where they would be visible) as an expanding set of concentric rings.

Of all the aspects of the original series, though, none required more work than the characters themselves. The principal figures of the series are charming, but they were created in the late 30's, and thus were quite dated. For instance, Joan Randall was more demure than a woman in her position would be today, while Curt Newton's ofttimes condescending attitude toward her left much to be desired. My task was to keep them and the other major characters as essentially the same individuals they'd been before, while also making them less...well, annoying. So Joan Randall, girl agent of the Planet Police, became Lt. Joan Randall, intelligence officer for Section 4 of the Interplanetary Defense Force. Otho, the android created by Roger Newton before his murder, was given both a new purpose in life and a reason for his strange name: Orthogenic Trans-Human Organism. Simon Wright, aka "the Brain", became a full-fledged cyborg, not just a disembodied brain floating in a box. And, Grag was upgraded to an intelligent robot, an accidental step forward in cybernetic evolution, a machine seeking to learn the human condition.

As for Curt himself, his character was deepened considerably, given a personal dimension that didn't exist before. When we meet him, he's not yet a hero, but instead a rather naïve young man who's lived most of his twenty years of life in isolation on the Moon, kept in hiding since infancy after the murder of his parents. No longer an omni-competent super-scientist and infallible hero, he's not your grandfather's Captain Future.

≈

I ORIGINALLY INTENDED for *Avengers of the Moon* to be the first volume of a trilogy, to be followed by *The Guns of Pluto* and *The Horror at Jupiter* (the last an homage to the original title of the first Captain Future novel). Unfortunately, very shortly after I turned in the final revisions of *Avengers of the Moon* to David Hartwell, my editor at Tor, David died in a tragic household accident. The young editor who succeeded David was less enamored with Captain Future than he had been; indeed, before she was given *Avengers of the Moon* to line-edit, she had no idea who the character was or his place in SF's history. I'm not sure she even liked space opera, or at least not the variety I'm writing. So, she killed the next two books, despite the fact that *Avengers* had favorable reviews, positive reader response, and solid sales in all its editions. No other publisher was interested in continuing a trilogy whose first volume was published by someone else.

I'd just about given up on Captain Future, and thought I'd never write another story about him again when the unexpected happened. My friend Steve Davidson, whom I knew from the New England SF convention circuit, acquired the rights to the long-defunct *Amazing Stories* and decided to revive it as a print magazine. When he approached me for a story for the first issue, I knew exactly what to offer him: the novella "Captain Future in Love," salvaged from *The Guns of Pluto,* which was half-finished when Tor nixed the second two books of the proposed trilogy.

"Captain Future" was serialized in the first two issues of the revived *Amazing,* and the response was positive enough that Steve offered me the chance to continue the series in his magazine. However, given the fact that I originally had a three-volume story arc in mind, it quickly became apparent that we'd have to run a Captain Future story in each and every issue of *Amazing* in order to tell this story. Obviously, we'd wear out Captain Future's welcome if we did that. But Steve is as much a pulp aficionado as I am, so our email conversation took a different direction and…well, here we are.

If you've never read any of Hamilton's original Captain Future novels or stories, don't worry; you won't need any prior knowledge of the series in order to enjoy this one. However, if you do want to read the originals, there are several ways to do so. There are a series of hardcover omnibus editions from Haffner Press, a series of trade-paperback facsimile reprints of the Better Publications *Captain Future* and *Startling Stories* from Adventure House, a series of ebook reprints from Altus Press, and even audio books from Radio Archives. And, of course, this series of new, authorized adventures: a pulp hero from the twentieth century, returning for the twenty-first.

The future is back. And his name is Captain Future.

About The Author

ALLEN MULHERIN STEELE, JR. became a full-time science fiction writer in 1988, following publication of his first short story, "Live From The Mars Hotel" (*Asimov's*, mid-Dec. 1988). Since then, he has become a prolific author of novels, short stories, and essays, with his work translated into more than a dozen languages worldwide.

Allen was born in Nashville, Tennessee. He received his B.A. in Communications from New England College in Henniker, New Hampshire, and his M.A. in Journalism from the University of Missouri in Columbia, Missouri. Before turning to SF, he worked as a staff writer for daily and weekly newspapers in Tennessee, Missouri, and Massachusetts, freelanced for business and general-interest magazines in the Northeast, and spent a short tenure as a Washington correspondent, covering politics on Capitol Hill.

His twenty-one novels include *Orbital Decay, Time Loves A Hero* (originally titled *Chronospace),* *V-S Day, Arkwright* and the Coyote series: *Coyote, Coyote Rising, Coyote Frontier, Coyote Horizon* and *Coyote Destiny;* and spin-off novels: *Spindrift, Galaxy Blues, Hex, Apollo's Outcast.* His first Captain Future novel, *Avengers of the Moon,* was published in 2017.

Allen's short fiction has appeared in most major American SF magazines, including *Asimov's Science Fiction, Analog,* and *Fantasy & Science Fiction,* as well as in dozens of anthologies. He has published seven short-fiction collections, including *Rude Astronauts, Sex and Violence in Zero-G: The Complete Near Space Stories,* and *Tales of Time and Space.*

His novella "The Death Of Captain Future" (*Asimov's,* Oct.1995) received the 1996 Hugo Award for Best Novella, won a 1996 *Science Fiction Weekly* Reader Appreciation Award, and received the 1998 Seiun Award for Best Foreign Short Story from Japan's National Science Fiction Convention. It was also a finalist for a 1997 Nebula Award by the Science Fiction and Fantasy Writers of America.

Allen's novella "…Where Angels Fear to Tread" (*Asimov's,* Oct./Nov. 1997) received the Hugo Award, the Locus Award, the *Asimov's* Readers Award, and the *Science Fiction Chronicle* Readers Award in 1998, and was a finalist for the Nebula, Sturgeon, and Seiun awards.

His novelette, "The Emperor of Mars" (*Asimov's,* June 2010) won the 2011 Hugo Award for Best Novelette and also the *Asimov's* Readers Award.

His novelette "The Good Rat" *(Analog,* mid-Dec. 1995) was a Hugo finalist in 1996, and his novelette "Zwarte Piet's Tale" (*Analog,* Dec. 1998) won an AnLab Award from *Analog* and was a Hugo finalist in 1999. His novelette "Agape Among the Robots" (*Analog,* May 2000) was a finalist for the Hugo in 2001. His novella "Stealing Alabama" (*Asimov's,* January 2001) was a Hugo finalist in 2002 and won the *Asimov's* Readers' Award for that year. His novelette "The Days Between" (*Asimov's* March 2001) was a Hugo finalist in 2002 and a Nebula finalist in 2003. His novella "Liberation Day" and novelette "The Garcia Narrows Bridge" both won the *Asimov's* Readers Awards in 2005. *Orbital Decay* received the 1990 Locus Award for Best First Novel, and *Clarke County, Space* was a finalist for the 1991 Philip K. Dick Award.

Allen was First Runner-Up for the 1990 John W. Campbell Award, received the Donald A. Wollheim Award in 1993, and the Phoenix Award in 2002. In 2013, he received the Robert A. Heinlein Award in recognition of his long career in writing space fiction.

He is a former member of both the Board of Directors and the Board of Advisers for the Science Fiction and Fantasy Writers of America, and is also a former adviser for the Space Frontier Foundation. In April, 2001, he testified before the Subcommittee on Space and Aeronautics of the US House of Representatives, in hearings regarding space exploration in the twenty-first century. "Live from the Mars Hotel" is among the many stories and novels included on the "Visions of Mars" disk aboard NASA's Phoenix lander, which landed on Mars in 2008.

Allen lives in western Massachusetts with his wife Linda and their dogs. You can find him on Facebook: <u>www.facebook.com/Allensteelesfwriter</u>

About the Cover Artist
Tony Sart

TONY SART, also known as Антон Яковлев, has been working in the gaming industry for over five years. Currently living in Moscow, Russia, he creates illustrations, promo-art, compositions, and concept art.

He can work in different styles and directions, and easily adapts to the necessary criteria. He enjoys working as part of a team and maintains high quality while working under tight deadlines. He started in a mobile games company, after which he went freelance, striving for more meaningful and complex projects.

You can see more of his art online at the following websites.

Tony Sart

tonysart.artstation.com
linkedin.com/in/tonysart
facebook.com/100010485393618

About the Interior Artist

M. D. Jackson

M.D. JACKSON is a Canadian science fiction, fantasy and horror artist and illustrator. He has been drawing since he was old enough to hold a pencil.

His artwork has appeared on numerous book covers, and in the pages of various magazines including the current revival of *Amazing Stories*. His artwork has been used on the covers of books from Pulpwork Press, Rogue Blades Press and Rage Machine Books, among others, and recently from The Experimenter Publishing Company.

His work has been featured on various websites including Darkworlds Quarterly. He was the co-publisher of *Darkworlds Quarterly Magazine* which he maintains, a non-fiction online publication, providing illustrations as well as design and layout of each issue. He also wrote many of the articles about science fiction, fantasy and art. He wrote about similar subjects for the Amazing Stories Magazine Website, as well as at the now defunct Heroicology Website. Before that, he was the co-publisher and art director of *Dark Worlds m*agazine, a pulp inspired print-on-demand fiction magazine. His work garnered him a co-nomination for a Pulp Ark Award in 2012.

He works mainly in a digital medium. Happily, he is also handy with an ink pen and, of course, that old tested and true technology of the HB pencil and a scrap of paper.

M. D. Jackson lives among the tall Douglas Firs in a small town in the wild lands of the interior of British Columbia. He lives with his wife and two cats. When not working, he passes the time by drinking beer and reading old books.

M.D. Jackson
mdjackson.artstation.com

About the Comet I/II Artist

Rob Caswell

WITH A FORMAL EDUCATION IN electro-mechanical drawing and astrophysics, Rob Caswell's scientific and science fiction illustration is the closest he gets these days to professionally applying his academic training. Rob has been a space hardware and cosmic adventure junkie since growing up in New Hampshire during the 60s space race, where he developed on a diet of *Space Angel* cartoons and Gerry Anderson TV shows.

Rob began his professional scifi illustration career in the eighties, primarily through paper-and-pen role-playing games (RPGs) such as *Traveller, Star Wars, Paranoia, 2300 A.D,, Space: 1889*, et al. He's also worked as a draftsman, comic book letterer, RPG editor and writer, computer game designer and artist, web designer, photo retoucher, digital printer, and illustrator for science fiction books. His artwork inspired the *Star Trek: Seekers* novel series by Simon & Schuster, for which he ultimately provided the cover art.

Meeting in the late 90s, Rob and Allen Steele formed a fast friendship over their numerous shared passions, dominated by science fiction and scale modeling. Rob has worked as an illustrator and designer of cover and interior technical illustrations on a number of Allen's projects, starting with the 2008 novel *Galaxy Blues*.

Rob crafted the design of the original Captain Future *Comet* which appeared inside *Avengers of the Moon*. Charged with the job of bringing the *Comet II* to life – Captain Future's succeeding set of cosmic wheels after the first ship's demise – Rob tried to both channel the Space-X and Scaled Composites inspired design ethos he'd applied to the original while taking it in a newer, grander direction. The result was a ship that dictated its own form from the loose details as it evolved in discussions and in the sketchbook, surprising both Rob and Allen with its final configuration.

Rob lives in Western Massachusetts in the foothills of the Berkshires, with is wife Deb Zeigler and a diverse variety of "wild guest/pets" buzzing, chirping, digging, grazing, and just passing through their woody yard. He currently operates Evolv Fine Art Printing – a giclée print studio in Easthampton, MA.

Rob Caswell
www.deviantart.com/rob-caswell

CAPTAIN FUTURE

The greatest space hero of science fiction's Golden Age, returns in this ALL NEW series of illustrated short novels written by multiple Hugo Award-winning author ALLEN STEELE, creator of the acclaimed Coyote series. Join Curt Newton and the Futuremen on an epic adventure that carries them from one side of the Solar System to the other... and beyond!

THE RETURN OF UL QUORN SERIES

BOOK 1 CAPTAIN FUTURE IN LOVE

BOOK 2 THE GUNS OF PLUTO

BOOK 3 1,500 LIGHT YEARS FROM HOME

COMING IN 2021 ... THE HORROR AT JUPITER

EPIC SPACE OPERA IN THE GRAND TRADITION!

The World's First Science Fiction Magazine

PRESENTS...

ADRIFT IN THE SEA OF SOULS

David Gerrold has been exploring the bizarre, the wonderful, and the horrific for more than half a century, with each new adventure expanding the event horizons of the imagination. Here are three stunning stories that explore the outer reaches of possibility and the inner depths of the human soul

ADRIFT IN THE SEA OF SOULS — *they call themselves travelers, hopping from body to body, from life to life, but in reality they are body-snatchers. Who are they and what do they want from the stranger who fell into their world?*

THE WHITE PIANO — *In a locked away room, hidden under a sheet, rests a faded old piano. In its glory days it was dazzling white with gold trim, but now in war-torn England, its paint is gray and peeling. No one is allowed to go near it, but sometimes after midnight, a lonely little girl still hears beautiful music.*

JACOB IN MANHATTAN — *A sequel chapter to the award-winning horror novel, Jacob, this savage novella shows how dangerous it can be to enrage a vampire. Not recommended for the squeamish or anyone under thirty, contains some graphic sex and violence. Don't read this at bedtime.*

A MASTER OF AMAZING FICTION INVITES YOU ABOARD!

David Gerrold has been writing professionally for half a century. He created the tribbles for "Star Trek" and the Sleestaks for "Land Of The Lost." His most famous novel is "The Man Who Folded Himself." His semi-autobiographical tale of his son's adoption, "The Martian Child" won both the Hugo and the Nebula awards, and was the basis for the 2007 movie starring John Cusack and Amanda Peet. His latest novel, Hella, is available at your local booksellers.

www.amazingstories.com

WHAT DOES A FUTURE WITHOUT POLICE LOOK LIKE?

In 2020, protesting citizens issued the cry to "defund the police." But what does that mean?

We challenged science fiction authors the world over to give us their vision of a world without police and fair systems of justice. In this collection you'll find eleven stories showing alternate forms of law enforcement and criminal justice spread across near future, alternate realities and different worlds. Explore places where everyone in the community takes a part to bring justice to killers and citizens step into the role of Mr. Rogers to be good neighbors and resolve disputes. Find worlds where the errant are helped to redemption and a future where a modern angst-ridden cop's mind is blown.

This anthology shows you what "defund the police" can look like. We invite you to take a journey into social landscapes you may not have thought possible.

READ AT YOUR OWN RISK!

A man whose spirit can hop from body to body tries to stay ahead of an organization that would exploit his ability for their own dark purposes. A young woman who discovers that her father had created a time machine has to use it to investigate his murder...and save the world from ecological catastrophe. Captain Future and the Futuremen become involved in what appears to be a simple case of sabotage that turns out to be the opening move of a plan for revenge put into motion by their greatest foe: Ul Quorn.

These are some of the exciting books that you will find from Amazing Selects.

Amazing Selects is a line of books which is being produced by Experimenter Publishing Company, LLC, the publisher of Amazing Stories magazine. Each volume includes a short novel by one of the premier authors in the science fiction field today, as well as additional fiction and non-fiction. Current publications include: Adrift in the Sea of Souls by David Gerrold; Tiny Time Machine by John Stith; and the on-going series The Return of Ul Quorn, by Allen Steele.

Amazing Selects books also includes No Police = Know Future, a collection of ten speculative fiction stories, inspired by contemporary protests, that imagine futures where alternatives to current policing practices have been developed to deal with criminal activity and personal disputes.

FOOLISH HUMANS - VISIT...

STORE.AMAZINGSTORIES.COM